IT'S
ALL
ABOUT
YOU

Unlocking Your Potential
to Achieve Success in
Every Aspect of Your Life

Robert Mesmer

Order this book online at www.trafford.com
or email orders@trafford.com

Most Trafford titles are also available at major online book retailers.

Printed in Victoria, BC, Canada.

ISBN: 978-1-4269-0725-8 (soft)
ISBN: 978-1-4269-0726-5 (hard)
ISBN: 978-1-4269-0727-2 (ebook)

*Our mission is to efficiently provide the world's finest, most comprehensive book publishing
service, enabling every author to experience success. To find out how to publish your
book, your way, and have it available worldwide, visit us online at www.trafford.com*

Trafford rev. 11/18/2009

 www.trafford.com

North America & international
toll-free: 1 888 232 4444 (USA & Canada)
phone: 250 383 6864 ♦ fax: 812 355 4082

To my wife, Gayle,

who is always doing for others.

How fortunate I am to know you, to love you.

To my sons, Jason and Chris.

You bring me such joy, such pride.

CONTENTS

INTRODUCTION

More and more people are actively pursuing success—they are "getting it" and "using it" to achieve the relationships, the goals, the lives they so desire. Yet the greater percentage of people feel they are at a standstill, a plateau, and have "hit the wall" in their personal or professional lives. Most ideas and dreams they have seem to be unattainable.

I want you to be honest with yourself when you answer this question: How many times in your life have you met or read about someone that you think truly has everything? These people have it all—happiness, health, friends, and financial success. They complete and succeed everything they attempt. They excel at everything they take part in. They seem to draw to themselves all the breaks and opportunities. Why do these people have it all? Why do some people succeed at everything they do while others continually fail? What are they doing that the average person is not?

Now you can unlock the secret of these thousands of success stories and apply it to yourself, in either your personal or professional life. You already have the tools to accomplish your goals. You have always had these tools. All humans are born with the tools to succeed. This gives us one step up on every other living thing on this earth. It would appear, then, that everyone would use these tools to achieve their goals.

It seems that anything we have been born with, that we have not had to earn, we take for granted. Our five senses of sight, taste, hearing, smell, and touch seem to reach their maximum value only when they have deteriorated or we have completely lost one of them. I have spent frustrating periods of time looking for my reading glasses, and I know I am not alone. This was time wasted when I could have been doing something else. As I look for my glasses again, I think how lucky I was to have had perfect eyesight for so many years. We are born with the ability to think, to reason, to imagine. We have not had to earn it; it is there for us.

It had long come to my attention that people of accomplishment rarely sat back and let things happen to them. They went out and happened to things.

Leonardo da Vinci

1

Success

Think of the term "success." What does it mean to you? Does being successful mean being rich? Does it mean being famous, or popular, or happy? Many people are not rich, famous, or popular, but are happy. Success, then, must be an individual mindset. Successful people live their lives in happiness and, as a result, their relatives, their friends, and their colleagues experience more joy than sorrow.

Success is a result of setting a standard, holding yourself to it, and controlling what you focus on. You create your life instead of just living it. Remember, we become what we think about. Our dominant thoughts, whether positive or negative, become our future. Successful people enjoy their lives and do not dwell on the past or the future, but enjoy the present.

successful people enjoy their life

Why do successful people prosper in everything they do? They have surely had failures, mistakes along their paths to success, yet they continually seem to rebound to achieve their goals. There are qualities of character that are common to these achievers.

The Ten Attributes of Highly Successful People

1) Purpose—Focus and direction occupy their minds; they know exactly what they want.

2) Passion—They love what they do; it's not just about the money.

3) Persistence—People who are successful never give up.

4) Discipline—They are well organized and willing to sacrifice niceties.

5) Refusal to compromise—Successful people do not tolerate mediocre achievement or incompetence.

6) Courage—They are courageous against adversity; it does not stop them.

7) People skills—They possess the ability to work with many types of people.

8) Wisdom—People who are successful are always consumed with learning and applying new ideas.

9) Decisiveness—They can make decisions when they need to.

10) Humor—A successful person has a sense of humor and knows when to use it.

1) **Purpose:** To get to where you want to be in your life requires focus and purpose. You can spend hours, days, weeks, and even years only to miss what you are trying to achieve. This is what happens in many people's lives when they don't have direction. You must provide yourself with a clear and specific topic to focus on. Hold that idea as a regular and dominant thought. Your subconscious mind is a powerful goal-achieving machine that will lead you to success.

2) **Passion:** People who succeed are passionate about what they do. They work longer and harder and give more attention

to their work than people without passion do. When other people would retire because they have made more money than they could ever spend, truly passionate people continue working, not for the money but because they love what they do.

3) **Persistence:** To achieve, to excel—to succeed—requires perseverance. Success gurus contend that the number one quality necessary to success is persistence. A successful person is persistent in striving for the final goal, and not necessarily in the method of getting there. Many of the great inventors we owe so much to today were persistent in their dreams even after many failures.

4) **Discipline:** Successful people pledge themselves to a course of action and stick to it. If you want to be a success, make a commitment to yourself; this is the most important discipline of all. There will be distractions along the way, but being disciplined means doing what you have to do on occasion even when you don't want to. It may even mean giving up an activity you enjoy to move ahead. With self-discipline,you will adhere to a time-management schedule that will enable you to meet your goal.

5) **Refusal to compromise:** We almost expect to find the word "uncompromising" in the mission statements of most successful companies. To be firm, unbending, and inflexible in the pursuit of quality brings credibility and respect to these companies. To succeed, you as an individual will want to be uncompromising with respect to your performance. You cannot settle for being mediocre, for just getting the job done, but must excel in every effort, every subgoal along the way. You are the product and you are completely responsible for not settling for anything less than peak performance.

6) **Courage:** Successful people have a quality of mental toughness. They can stand up to adversity, for it will not stop them. They are able to accept criticism and resist personal attack. If you want to be successful, you must have the courage to win. The CEOs and the MVPs of the world possess the ability to perform under pressure and to triumph. They excel in high-pressure situations and have a mental edge over their competitors. Confidence and resilience are qualities evident in these leaders. You can be one of these people. It is completely up to you.

7) **People Skills:** The most important attribute is also the attribute that is the easiest to improve upon—good people skills. Much of what happens to you in your life has to do with other people. I can recall a superintendent in a district of 1500 teachers. When he visited a school in his district, he would know all the teachers by their first names. He always wanted to hear what someone had to say, whether it was personal or job-related. As well as being a listener, he was a doer. Needless to say, he was very well respected and had the ability to rally the troops. He was a success.

8) **Wisdom:** Successful people have open minds and are always ready to learn. They are open to suggestions, solutions, and new information. They realize the value of another perspective. When you think you know all there is to know, you stop growing as an individual. Successful people never stop growing. They take the time to study, and to develop their skills in new or related areas.

9) **Decisiveness:** How many times have you missed an opportunity because you couldn't make a decision or make one fast enough? Some people don't make decisions because they are afraid to make the wrong decision and fail. Successful people, right or wrong, make decisions. It is better to have

tried and failed than not to have tried at all. You learn from your mistakes. You make decisions every day; it's a part of your life.

10) **Sense of Humor:** A sense of humor is not only essential in everyday life, but beneficial to success in business as well. Too many people take life too seriously. The next time you watch an interview with Richard Branson, note that he is a person with not only a passion for what he does, but also a great sense of humor. He is constantly smiling. Laughter is a great stress antidote.

We are built to conquer the environment, solve problems, achieve goals, and we find no real satisfaction or happiness in life without obstacles to conquer and goals to achieve.

Maxwell Maltz

2

Setting Successful Goals

The functional structure of any successfully achieved goal starts at the goal and backs up to the seed. Whether the goal is long- or short-term, there is a beginning and an ending. The vision of being a teacher or running in the marathon may be the major goal, the ending, but that goal requires steps that become evident the more one pursues it. For example, to be a teacher, you will need an education degree.

> imagine yourself at your goal then back up

To get the degree, you may have to attend a university for a five-year period. To pay for the university fees and living expenses, you have to work in the summer and maybe part time in the winter as well. To run the marathon, you need to prepare your body and increase its endurance. To prepare your body, you will need to follow a dedicated training and eating schedule. Successfully achieved goals are the outcome of imagining yourself at your goal and then backing up to the beginning, which is determined by your situation in life at the point of creating your goal. You then move forward toward your goal, beginning with short-term goals that will help you achieve your major goal. If, at all times, you carry the vision of achieving your goal, the required steps along the way will fall into place. Achieving your goal is all a matter of "baby steps."

Setting a goal is taking your imagination and motivating yourself to turn a vision into reality. If this idea is as simple as it seems, why do so many people fail to reach their goals while others continually succeed? The successful goal setters follow a plan.

FIVE COMPONENTS TO SUCCESSFULLY ACHIEVING GOALS

It's all about D-R-I-V-E. Do you have the drive to achieve your goals, or are you missing a component?

D—Definition

R—Realism

I—Inscription

V—Visualization

E—Emotion

Definition—Successfully achieving a goal starts here. Too many people fail to reach their goals because they do not define them correctly. To achieve your goal, you must first define it and then narrow it down. You must be absolutely clear as to what goal you want to reach. You must know what you want before you can go after it. How did you arrive at this goal? Did you watch a person or an event that impressed you so much that your creative juices started **define your smallest sub goals for your present reality** flowing? The light went on, but what or who flipped the switch? Knowing how you came up with your goal will help you define it more precisely. Once you understand your major goal, you need to break it down into subgoals (babysteps). These subgoals will help you stay on the right path and give you confidence and immediate focus as you achieve each one. Small-action goals or steps will lead to major results. Defining your goals, big and small, is necessary to starting on a clear and organized path. Immediate is the key word here. (Refer to chapter 29 on time.) You control your focus at the moment. The only thing that exists is the present. The past is a memory and the future exists in your imagination, so define your smallest subgoals for your present reality. A present-reality subgoal might be meeting with a university counselor to learn exactly what is required to become a heart surgeon. You may want to go to the motor vehicle branch to find the requirements to get your driver's license endorsed for air brakes for commercial truck driving. It doesn't matter what your interest is; there are immediate subgoals. Defining subgoals will enhance your present reality. You will be inspired, because you have actually taken immediate action. As you reach each of your present-reality goals, you will find that your major or long-range goal will be that much easier to see in your imagination because you know you are doing rather than just dreaming.

You may want to ask yourself if your work is just a job to support yourself. Have you really thought about what you want from life? Have you ever written anything down? Define your goals and establish clarity.

Realism—You want to be successful, so it is important for you to set realistic goals that you can actually achieve. Your goal should be realistically attainable. When you have no chance of reaching a goal, your motivation, enthusiasm, and confidence will be diminished. A two-hundred-pound person should not harbor visions of becoming a professional jockey. This may seem obvious, but many goals are in a grey area. People who take honest, accurate assessments of themselves are well on their way to creating realistic goals. Throughout your life, many other people (parents, teachers, employers) have set goals for you, presumably all with good intentions. These goals may be unrealistic for you if they have not considered your interests or ambitions. Your passion may be lacking and this lack will thwart your chances of success. Start by setting an attainable goal in your mind.

Many people never reach their short-term or long-term goals because they have set them too high. A young student of mine came to see me one day, quite discouraged. He wanted to run a marathon. On his first day of training, he went out and ran ten miles. The following day, he could barely walk. He had set his immediate short-term goal too high for his physical condition. A week later, he was under proper progressive training with a knowledgeable coach.

People also fail by making their goals too easy. There is almost a direct correlation between the level of difficulty of a goal and the satisfaction a person gets from achieving it. When the goal seems unimportant, a person may put less effort into achieving it, even though it may be a stepping-stone to a more significant goal.

Inscription—Writing your goals down on paper is imperative. You now have physical evidence of what you are thinking. You are already completing the first step toward your major goal. The act of writing your goal on paper, or typing it on your computer, completes a subgoal. You are now organizing your imagination, a very powerful step. Writing your goal will give you satisfaction and improve your life now, not tomorrow. There is only now; you can live only in the now, not the

you may plan your future but you will always live in the present

future. You may plan the future, but you will always live in the present.

You may be a well-organized person in your mind, but committing your goals to paper adds a number of advantages. A flowchart of your goal with its subgoals will bring clarity to your project and can be revisited again and again. You can alter your goals; remember, they are written in ink, not stone. Your written goals will serve as a measuring tool. Are you meeting, completing your subgoals? Are you keeping to the schedule you set for yourself? The written goals will encourage you to be honest with yourself. Are you making the effort, taking the action, sacrificing the time required to complete the task? Writing a goal and its subgoals will greatly enhance a discussion with a colleague, a parent, or a friend. It can be very beneficial to hear another's comments on your thoughts, although it's entirely up to you, as it always is, as to whether you want to share them.

Visualization—Since the beginning of time, everything that man has created has begun as an imaginary idea, a visualization. The amazing accomplishments of man—landing on the moon, for example, or flying five hundred people through the sky comfortably at five hundred miles per hour—began as thoughts. This visualization leads to desire and passion, which in turn lead to action.

This key component to realizing your goals is something you have always had and you use everyday. Has anyone ever told you that you are a dreamer? Dreams are fine, but they are just fantasies, unless you act upon them. Now imagine shaping and directing these dreams and ideas to a specific target. As well as writing down your goals, however small or large they might be, it is imperative to be able to see them clearly in your mind so you can carry them with you. We think in pictures, so create with pictures.

Some people find it quite difficult in the beginning to keep their visualizations in their minds, or conjure them up at any time. Thousands of people have had great success by building visual flowcharts. To create your flowchart, place actual pictures of goals or subgoals on a wall or bulletin board. These can be pictures of people, places, articles—anything pertinent to your goal. See chapter 31 on "PPB." A technique I have

> **we think in pictures so create with pictures**

found to be very effective for weight loss is the building of two such vision boards. You will need two previous pictures of yourself at the desired weight. If you don't have any, create them. Take a pair of scissors, two pictures of yourself, and two pictures from a magazine of a body size resembling your desired outcome. Cut the heads off your photos and paste them on these new bodies. You need two because you should place one on the fridge and one on your bathroom mirror. You are now "inputting" the image into your brain everytime you glance at them, which will be several times a day. Within a couple of days, you will be able to go anywhere with that image clearly stored in your brain and to "go to it" instantly. This technique is certainly not limited to weight loss. This is very powerful stuff; do not underestimate its value. Refer to chapter 17 on Imagination.

Emotion—Emotion, enthusiasm, passion, whatever you want to call it, is a prime ingredient in reaching any worthwhile goal. To become successful, just look at what the major players are doing that others are not. What is it that makes some people succeed at what they do while others continually fail? They have a genuine passion and love for their work. Donald Trump, Bill Gates, and Warren Buffet all have a passion for what they do; otherwise, they would have stopped years ago. Whatever goal you are setting, whether it be a short- or long-term goal, ask yourself if you are truly passionate and excited about it.

Make up your mind right now to succeed and the odds are definitely in your favor. When you create goals that are not of value to you, you may find it difficult to achieve them. When you become enthusiastic about certain ideas, which are really goals, you will actually help yourself to accomplish them. Enthusiasm creates action.

In any moment of decision, the best thing you can do is the right thing, the next best thing is the wrong thing, and the worst thing you can do is nothing.

Theodore Roosevelt

3

Decision Making

The choices, or decisions, you make govern your entire life. You are where you are today because of the decisions you made in the past. Have you made the right decisions? Are you completely happy with the choices you've made? The research indicates that you are probably not. I have yet to meet the person who is completely satisfied with every decision he or she has made. This person does not exist. We learn by our mistakes, but with only one run-through of life, we would like there to be as few mistakes as possible.

where you are today is a result of the decisions you made in the past

The number of decisions you make everyday would probably surprise you, as you make most of them without consciously thinking that you are making a choice. The moment you awaken, you begin to choose. What will I have for breakfast? Which clothes will I wear today? Should I get gas on the way to work? Will that be paper or plastic? Credit or debit? Should I lease a car and invest the money I have saved or buy a car and not have those monthly payments?

The small decisions amazingly define our lives. A teaching colleague of mind related how a tiny decision altered his life completely. He was driving to the next town to seek his first teaching position. There were several cars in front of him as he came up to the intersection. The light turned red and as he sat there in traffic, he glanced over to the left and saw a school. Instead of staying in line, he decided to turn into the parking lot and check the hiring status of the school. They were looking for a teacher with his credentials. He got the job and spent the first nine years of his career at that particular school. He says that if there had not been traffic, if he had not pulled into that school, if the school hadn't hired him, he would have taught in a different part of the country, married someone else, and had different children. A different life—all from heavy traffic at the intersection!

The desire you imagine is the seed, your occasional closing of the eyes in imagery is the sun, and your constant, though not anxious, expectation is the rain and cultivation necessary to bring absolutely sure results.

Francis Larimer Warner

4

The Law of Attraction

Althoughyou may not know or completely understand the law of attraction, you have been using it for your entire existence, and you will continue to do so. When you understand this law, you can harness it, direct it, and feed it to achieve success. It is the single most important concept in understanding why one person fails and another succeeds.

You attract into your life people, events, or activities that coincide with your thoughts. The stronger the thought, the greater the emotion, the more likely it is that the attraction will enter your life. The law of attraction is exactly that, a law, a natural force that doesn't waiver, doesn't budge. It works on the same principle every time. What you attract in your life is completely up to you.

> you attract your dominant thoughts that carry the greatest emotions

Dominant thoughts carry the greatest emotions. The law of attraction does not determine if the emotions are positive or negative, or whether these thoughts are right or wrong. There is only one person that makes that decision, and that person is you.

When you let doubt enter your mind, you will surely fail. The law of attraction is at work. Think back to incidents, no matter how small, in your life. If you think about how they came about, you will see the law in action.

As I look back upon my early life, I see examples of the law of attraction. When I was six, I caught the bus downtown with my brother, who was nine at the time. It was a big thrill, as it was the first time without my parents. We didn't live far from town, so it was only a fifteen minute ride. The bus driver's name was Freddy, and he knew everybody. He was laughing and talking all the way to town. He knew my parents, and from then on when I rode his bus, he referred to me as Bobby. Freddy obviously loved his job because he loved people. He told me once that it was just like picking up his friends each day. I always sat at the very front so I could talk to him and watch him drive that big bus. The pedals were big and made out of metal. The brake pedal made a hiss when he took his foot off of it. *How cool is this, picking up your friends and driving this bus,* I thought to myself. *When I grow up, I would like to be a bus driver.*

My young mind was racing, imagining how much fun it would be to drive the bus and pick up people. That day was the beginning of a law of attraction. Fourteen years later, I had just finished my first year of university and was looking for a summer job. Still in the back of my mind was the desire to drive a bus. The regular transit drivers were taking holidays with their families, and the bus company needed summer drivers. I applied and got the job. I was a little nervous but very excited. The first day, there were six of us standing in the garage waiting for road training. Our instructor for the road training was none other than Freddy. Although he had retired, he was back as an instructor for the summer students. I'll never forget that job and how much I enjoyed going to work each day.

We may become attracted to negative situations quite innocently, due to our untrained minds. Many people believe that thinking just happens and give no practice, time, or direction to it. But you can train your mind not to accept negative thoughts, and to dwell on the positive. You will begin to draw to yourself positive people and situations because you are now dominating your thoughts with controlled, positive images.

Every man's memory is his private literature.

Aldous Huxley

5

Remember Your Memory

In both your personal and professional lives, quiet confidence and success come from having a good memory. Many people are content with having average memories or even squeezing by with poor ones. Successful people have good memories and continue to exercise and develop them. You can improve your memory; all that is necessary is a little organization.

Your memory is the meat of your existence. Your brain handles each individual memory according to its relevance, its emotional rating, and your decision. The brain handles memory in three categories: sensory memory, short-term memory (STM), and long-term memory (LTM).

SENSORY MEMORY

Sensory memory is what you react to immediately from any one of your five senses. It only lasts for a second or two. You look at the direction sign in the airport and turn right, toward departures. Someone asks you a question, and you respond. Although it may be a split second before you react, during that time, you are remembering what you just saw or what you just heard.

SHORT-TERM MEMORY (STM)

Your short-term memory storage is for information you are processing and is often referred to as the "working memory," similar to RAM in your computer. When you read something, you need to retain it long enough to understand it. Have you ever read a couple of sentences without retaining them and read them again for understanding? Short-term memory is

> **enhance your retention with chunking**

limited and decays rapidly. You can enhance your retention by "chunking" information. When you can group certain parts of a piece of information, you can increase your capacity. Phone numbers are chunked by breaking up the ten digits into the area code, the prefix, and finally, the last four. It is in short-term memory that you decide whether or not to transfer the information to long-term storage in your brain.

LONG-TERM MEMORY (LTM)

Long-term memory can last a few days or a lifetime. This is where your entire life's log is stored. You decide whether to pass information from short to long-term storage. The duration of retention of information, of course, depends on the individual. Most people cannot remember any information before the age of three. Recent studies have concluded that memory retention is enhanced with emotional arousal, be it either positive or negative.

All memory is based on association. Anything new you wish to remember must be associated with something you already remember. You are associating right now about what you have just read. When you remember a person's name, you are associating the name with the face. When you remember a quote, you are associating it with a visual image of that product or service. Do you remember a time when you have said to yourself or a colleague, "Oh yes, that reminds me!" The association may not be evident with this recall of information, but it is there. Much of the time, associations are made

> **all memory is based on association**

subconsciously. Conscious associations are the result of a trained memory. You used conscious association at a very early age. Do you remember learning "i before e except after c" to spell correctly, or "Every Good Boy Deserves to have Fun" to learn the music staff? If you understand associations and training your mind to make them, you will be amazed at what your memory can do for you.

ASSOCIATE NEW TO OLD

Once you understand how association works, you can apply it to your own life and almost instantly achieve amazing results. Most people who were old enough can remember where they were when JFK was assassinated, or when Lady Diana died in the car accident, or when the twin towers were hit. These major events have major emotions tied to them, which strengthen the associations. You may simply connect the memory to where you were or to an event in your life that occurred at that time. You were associating new memory to old memory.

You can now organize and train your memory, using this key to unlock an amazing ability to remember lists, names, quotes, facts, history, or in fact, anything you want to remember. Research tells us that most people, on average, can remember five to seven items on a list before having to write them down. Test yourself and see how you stack up against the average. Try this with a friend: Ask your friend to compile a list of ten different objects and then read the list to you slowly, one item after the other. Wait five minutes and write down as many as you can. How did you do? How would you like to do this everytime, twice as fast, with twenty objects and with 100 percent recall, in or out of order?

To start with, you will need to have a home base of "pegs" with which you are most familiar. The "pegs" are different locations, already in your memory bank, that you can see in your mind readily. The one home base that you are familiar with would be your own body; another might be your house or apartment. You can even build a home base by memorizing key words to numbers. Your body is a great homebase to start with.

Here is a list of ten everyday objects to memorize with your new skill of association with an already-known and easy-to-visualize "peg." Follow the instructions right after the list to memorize these items as quickly as possible.

1) Umbrella

2) Old red VW beetle.

3) Bottle of Scotch

4) Mattress

5) Baby buggy

6) Salmon

7) Elephant

8) Computer

9) Bus

10) Kitchen sink

The more ridiculous the association, the easier it is to recall. Start with your head as number one: picture a giant umbrella balancing on the top of your head, but upside down. Go immediately to your left shoulder and picture yourself holding up the side of the VW beetle with your shoulder while someone is dragged out from underneath it. Now go to your right shoulder and see a bottle balancing precariously on top of your shoulder; it doesn't even have to say "Scotch" on it; your mind will automatically remember this tidbit. Go to your left hand

> **the more ridiculous the association the easier it is to recall**

and close it; open it to see a little miniature mattress. Now see yourself leaning over a bridge, holding in your right hand a baby buggy with a baby in it; the only thing preventing it from falling is your right hand. Look down at your waist now, which is number six, and you can see a bunch of gigantic fish hanging from your belt; what a catch! Now look at your left knee as you knee the elephant in the behind and send him flying into the air. As you look at your right knee, which is now stuck inside a broken computer screen, look down at your left foot, which has just been run over by a bus and is completely flattened out. Your other foot, the right one, is too big to get in the kitchen sink to wash.

It's easy to remember your body parts as numbers by using your head as number one and going down, using a left-to-right scheme. You can add or delete parts to suit your list.

Take a piece of paper and write down the numbers 1 through 10, and beside each number, the object. Is it not amazing how these objects all came back to you, and in order? You can recall them out of order as well, or even backward. When you have a list and you do need to have them numbered or in a particular order, you do not have to have a home base. You can simply link the list together. The umbrella might be held in place of the VW's ragtop because it is leaking because of the gigantic bottle of scotch that is sticking out of the backseat as you are trying to soak up the mess with a mattress. I am sure that now you can finish off the rest of the associations.

Whether you think you can or whether you think you can't, you are right.

Henry Ford

6

Let's Get Physical

The imagination process created in your brain can be greatly enhanced. Your brainpower can be improved upon by using it. In infancy and early childhood, your brain goes through changes from its initial sorting of experience. Your five senses transfer external stimuli into electrical impulses traveling from one neuron to another. As a skill is developed, these neuron routes become more pronounced, and become faster and easier for the brain to follow. These skills can be in the physical realm, such as writing your name, swinging a bat, or putting on a shoe. Thought processes also are strengthened when you make a deduction or a decision, or even improve upon a mental image you have created.

Our brains continue to grow throughout our lives as long as we continue to experience new things. An MRI (brain imaging) can actually take a picture of areas of the brain getting more blood at a certain period, correlating the change with the task or state of emotion or imagining something. Making these changes are what our brains

changes come about when you think new thoughts

were designed to do. Changes come about when you think new thoughts, and thoughts are imagination. Our ability to effect change in our brains through imagination is directly related to our drive and desire to leave our comfort zones.

*The mind of man is capable
of anything because
everything is in it, all the
past as well as the future.*

Joseph Conrad

7

The Left-Brain/Right-Brain Phenomenon

Our modern medical technology has produced brain-scanning systems like the MRI, or magnetic resonance imaging, and the PET, positron emission tomography, allowing us almost to see the brain in operation. As you do or think about different things, the scanners show,through colors lighting up, which parts of the brain are becoming active.

LEFT-BRAIN FUNCTIONS	RIGHT-BRAIN FUNCTIONS
Reality-based	Control imagination
Use logic	Risk-taking
Acknowledge	Special perception
Safe	Use feeling
Practical	Recognize symbols and images
Detail-oriented	Relate present to future
Fact-based	Big-picture-oriented
Control words and language	Control belief
Form strategies	Control appreciation
Relate present to past	Deal with philosophy and religion
Control comprehension	
Math- and science-related	Know object function
Can perceive order	Fantasy-based
Assign and remember object names	Impetuous

Although your brain has two hemispheres, which operate well independently and have different functions, they are amazingly interconnected and work together in seamless harmony.

THE LEFT-BRAIN/RIGHT-BRAIN CREATIVE PROCESS

In 1945, G. Wallis, in his book *The Art of Thought*, divided the creative process into four stages. The first stage, the *preparation*, was the gathering of information relating to the problem. The second stage was the *incubation* period in which the problem was handed to the subconscious mind. During the *incubation period,* you could continue to consciously think about the problem but put no pressure on yourself for a conclusion. The *illumination* stage may create a possible

you have experienced the illumination stage

solution and may come instantly, or an hour, or even a day, later. You have probably experienced this stage in the middle of the night when an idea or solution has come to you. You have intuition that at this point may produce a possible solution. In the fourth and final stage, *verification,* these intuitive solutions are held up against logic, and altered, if need be, to a workable solution.

The first and last stages—*preparation* and *verification*—are left-brain activities which we have been taught since early childhood. The middle stages—*incubation* and *illumination*—are not as easily defined as they are subconscious activities.

Creative individuals learn to rely on their intuition at this point, favoring diagrams, sketches, and physical movement over verbal thinking. Most problem solvers can best achiever creative activity by generating ideas non-verbally and using verbal thinking to verify them. The basis of successful creativity is the bonding relationship of the left and right brain. As much as you are dependent on the right brain for a creative idea, you are equally dependent on the left brain for logically determining its validity.

Your subconscious mind is always reproducing according to your habitual mental patterns.

Joseph Murphy

8

Two Minds Hand in Hand

There is a very popular belief that each mind is actually two minds, the conscious and the subconscious. The understanding of how these two minds work together will help clarify the role of the imaginative process in achieving the things we desire in life.

THE CONSCIOUS MIND

When you first learned to tie your shoelaces, it was a very proud moment, but an awkward one. You consciously had to think about it. You were using your conscious mind. Each time you tied your shoes, you became more skilled, and gradually it became "second nature" to you. It then became a part of your subconscious mind and you now do it almost automatically. You can be watching TV, talking to someone on the phone, or focusing on something completely different, all while tying your shoe.

My lessons on the golf tee have been much like this. As a beginner, I was consciously trying to remember all the tips at once. I should keep my chin up and my arm straight, bend at

our conscious mind is our logical thinking mind

the knees, hold the club like a bird, and on and on. I used my conscious mind to develop all these skills by focused repetition, working toward completing the swing without even thinking about it. *Just swing through the ball without thinking about it.* When Icould do this and do it consistently, I was beginning to use my subconscious mind.

The conscious mind is our thinking mind. It deducts and computes from external stimuli recorded by our five senses. It takes this data and stores it long term into the subconscious. Your conscious mind is organized, to a certain degree. It is logical and can analyze situations and make decisions accordingly. Your short-term memory is stored here. In fact, you are using your conscious mind as you read this. The person you just met two minutes ago is stored in your conscious mind.

THE SUBCONSCIOUS MIND

The subconscious runs our automatic nervous system. All the functions that run our body without our having to think consciously about them are taken care of by our subconscious mind. When we are hot, our bodies perspire to cool us off. When we are frightened or in high-stress situations, lactic acid is shot into our muscles to help us perform beyond anything we could consciously try on our own. You still can't outrun that grizzly, but you will probably complete your fastest hundred ever!

The subconscious mind is where our long-term memory is stored. Have you ever tried to consciously think of someone's name but can't recall it? You can see his or her face, but the name just isn't there. It's still in your subconscious and being called up. An hour later, it suddenly comes to you. All of your

our subconscious mind is our creative mind

past experiences, most of which cannot be recalled consciously, are still there in your subconscious mind.

Your creativity originates from this mind, which never rests. When you sleep at night, your conscious mind rests, but your subconscious does not. How many times have we heard someone say to us, referring to a problem or decision, "Let me sleep on it"? I quite often wake up at five in the morning with a great idea of how to solve a situation, or with a new idea to add to an article. Sometimes these notions or ideas are very brief and fleeting. If you have this experience, I would suggest writing the idea down so that you can return to a restful sleep. The mind may not settle for worry of forgetting it later upon awakening.

Just as you exercise any other muscle in your body to train it to perform at a higher level, you should exercise your brain. You exercise your conscious mind every day just by using it. At a young age, when you were learning your times tables, you were exercising your mind. Your mind learned, through trial and error, just how hard to throw the ball to achieve the distance. It even relayed to your arm and hand muscles where to position the glove to catch the ball, and at an amazing speed. Try writing that computer program! The subconscious mind, the creative part, can be exercised also. Set aside some time when you won't be disturbed and take yourself on an imaginary trip. It's like you are telling someone a bedtime story and you are making it up as you go along. Try to put some progression into it: Go up or down several floors in an elevator, then down a long hallway past several doors.

Open a door and create an interesting scene as you look around the room. Leave the story just as you came in by going back down the hallway and back into the elevator. See chapter 17 on developing your imagination.

9

The Individual You

There are billions of people on this earth but there is no one exactly like you. It is actually quite amazing. You are a true individual. The way you learn, the way you think, and the way you take action make you unique. Many people are unaware of their own best learning style. They have never really thought about or analyzed it. Do you feel you learn and absorb information best by seeing, hearing, or doing? Do you prefer to read instructions on your own or see a demonstration? Do you listen to how to do something or just get in there and learn while you are doing? Depending on the skill level and the actual activity, the learning experience can quite often involve a combination of all three. You will find, however, with some serious thought, that you favor, and excel in, one of the learning styles.

what is your learning style

I LIKE TO SEE

The most common learning style, of course, is that of visual individuals. They like to have the information in front of them. They are readers and observers. They like to see people rather than just talk to them on the phone. Slideshows, PowerPoint presentations, charts, graphs, videos, and pictures are their preferred methods of receiving information. A good thing to know about potential clients is what they are comfortable with.

I LIKE TO HEAR

Individuals who like to listen may favor the auditory learning style. They enjoy lectures, audio books, music, speeches, and seminars. They like visuals and ideas explained. They enjoy PowerPoint presentations and slideshows as long as there is verbal explanation to accompany them.

I LIKE TO DO

The types of people who like to learn by doing and shun the previous two learning styles are hands-on individuals. They do not want to sit in a classroom, but rather skip the instructions and get right into it. Trades that require physical dexterity attract people with this learning style. Such people are usually very good at their crafts because they have found what they are comfortable with, what they enjoy. Athletes, both professional and amateur, fall into this group—*I just want to get out on that field and play.* Enough instruction on your swing, already. Go out and hit some balls while your coach observes. *You can talk to me coach, but talk to me while I am skating.*

If doubt is challenging you and you do not act, doubts will grow. Challenge the doubts with action and you will grow. Doubt and action are incompatible.

John Kanary

10

What Creates Your Inhibitions?

Do you care what others think? Most of us do. However, when you become so concerned about how others think and view you, you place a limit on your performance. You will become self-conscious and too cautious in trying to make a good impression. Do you recognize any of the following inhibitive traits in your personality?

Do you suffer from any of the following?

- a shyness when in crowds or with members of the opposite sex

- a fear of public speaking

- insecurity and low self-esteem

- performance anxiety

- lack of self-confidence when interacting with people of authority

- social anxiety

- fear of other people resulting in lack of contact

- self-consciousness due to lack of self-assurance

- stage fright

- a lack of assertiveness and courage

- anxiety about taking tests or being the focus of attention

- self-doubt when expressing yourself in front of strangers

- a loss for words in stress situations

- a lack of self-confidence in meetings and negotiations

These are common examples of inhibitions that can make your life difficult and prevent you from achieving both personal and professional success.

You are perfectly normal if some of these traits fit your personality. You are certainly not alone. These psychological traits are normal patterns of behavior. Even though they are impractical patterns of conduct, once they have been learned and acquired, just like any other habit, they occur automatically without any conscious thought. They are a response system to life's interactions. Uninhibited people have an unrestricted and self-assured response. This allows them to react with confidence in any given situation. Your reaction in any situation is usually a consequence of your personal experience and upbringing.

These inhibitions can usually be traced back to acquired habits. Holding back emotions and not expressing them encourages an unconscious pattern of behavior. When I was in high school, I was quite inhibited regarding oral reports or even standing up in class to answer a question. I would do anything to avoid it. Even when I knew the answer, I would not put my hand up. A few years earlier, in elementary school, I had been just on the outside of a "clique" of boys. They

inhibitions can be traced back to acquired habits

were the popular ones who always did and said the right thing. I never seemed to say the right thing and so I said less and less. This was probably the beginning of my fear of speaking in any situation. Although I was totally unaware of it, I was developing a negative habit that would inhibit my success in life until I dealt with it.

It is time to break through the barriers that have held you back and held you down for such a long time. It's time to reach out and indelibly etch your place in history."

Greg Hickman

11

Are You A Spectator or A Player?

One of the most difficult challenges you face in the world is to change your outlook, your work ethic, and your ability to sacrifice something to achieve a better life. You can start by being honest with yourself; if you can't do that, then don't read the following questions. Are you a spectator or are you a player? Read the following ten questions and answer with a yes or no.

1) Are you one of the last few to volunteer in a group?

2) Do you watch TV two or more hours a day?

3) Do you play electronic games two or more hours a day?

4) Do you prefer watching instead of playing sports?

5) Have you ever felt guilty about not doing something for someone else?

6) Do you think it's better to just "fit in" rather than to standout?

7) Do other people intimidate you when you are trying something new?

8) Do you hesitate to participate unless you can be the best?

9) Do you hesitate to offer an opinion because people might disagree?

10) Have you thought about joining a club or organization, but never have?

Now that you have read and thought about the questions, add up your "yes" answers. If you had:

- 10—you are a dreamer rather than a doer.

- 7—9—you tell yourself you are going to do this and you are going to do that, but nothing ever seems to be accomplished.

- 5—7—you have made some action plans, started to move on them but have gotten sidetracked with some easier activity.

The more yes answers, the more you need to take control of your life.

If you want to be a player you can be a player. I have often been asked what the most important piece of advice is that I could give young people today to help them achieve their dreams. It would be to become a player, not a spectator. That also applies to adults; in fact, it applies to anyone who wants to achieve success. I can't imagine anyone who wouldn't want success and happiness. That does not mean that you can't watch TV, a movie, or you favorite sport. It means that you should try as many things as you can in your life:

sports, activities, games, organizations, lectures, and clubs. I have always firmly believed that we are all born with skills, talents, or natural ability above the norm in some area. Unfortunately, many people go through life unfulfilled because they never discovered their particular talents because they never experienced the activity. How many times have you heard "you don't know until you've tried"? That is a truism, for I have witnessed it time and time again.

When I was in my teens, we used to go as a family to a full-day logging fair every July.My mother was always keen to have us participate in everything. My father suggested to my mother that she try the nail-driving contest. We all laughed, but she entered and won!The following year, my father bought her a brand-new hammer just for the event. My mother came in last that year, but we respected her even more for becoming a player! It's the stuff life is made of.

To become a player may mean you are stepping out of your comfort zone, at least for a little while. When you find your strengths and unique form of talent, a surge of self-confidence and enthusiasm will enter your life. Develop these talents to the best of your ability. Do not settle for anything less. Do not let negativity or negative people enter your life.

opportunities abound from mistakes

Opportunities abound from mistakes, so step forward and don't be afraid to make a few along the way.Every single person on this earth is unique and has his or her own path to pursue. When you are on your path, you will know you are doing the right thing.

There is such an unlimited number of possibilities that one can easily be lost in the maze. You can offset the feeling of being overwhelmed by remaining focused on your dreams—the ideas that you feel comfortable with, that give you a feeling of enthusiasm and confidence.

Though no one can go back
and make a brand new start,
anyone can start from now
and make a brand new end.

Carl Bard

12

Are You Ready For Change?

What are you not doing, being, or having in your life that you want to do, be, or have? The answer to this question should give you a beginning to understanding what is missing and what you can do about it. Try to recall your last success or accomplishment. Do you remember that "feel-good" experience of achievement? You want to change, but you must be ready to change. The following test will help you assess what in your present personality or attitude is in need of change. No answer is completely right or wrong. Answer quickly with the first impression that comes to mind. In the space provided after the questions, place a 1, 2, or 3 for each of your choices.

A) You have just inherited $50,000 and decide to put it toward your accommodations.

   1) You move to a new rental.

   2) You renovate your house.

   3) You move to a new house.

B) You consider your forte to be:
1) That you are very creative.
2) That you can adapt to different situations.
3) That you are a very patient person.

C) Which of the following is your "Achilles' heel"?
1) I am impatient a lot of the time.
2) I dwell on the past.
3) I am very cautious.

D) If you had private counseling with a professional, which would you want to pursue in your personal life?
1) A new direction.
2) An improved state of mind.
3) Development.

E) You are in politics running for office. What might be your slogan?
1) It's Time for Change.
2) Working Together as One.
3) More Effort Creates Efficiency.

F) You are going to take a self-improvement course. Which would it be?
1) Communication Skills
2) Stress Management
3) Fitness

G) You are writing your first book. The title would be:

   1) *Think before You Leap*

   2) *Conflict Avoidance*

   3) *A New You*

H) When you have a major decision you prefer to:

   1) Consider others' opinions.

   2) Be confident in making a quick decision.

   3) Take your time going over your options.

I) You have been invited to a formal banquet. Your concern would be:

   1) That the party won't be interesting.

   2) That you won't be interesting.

   3) That you won't know anyone.

J) You are marooned on an island. Which would you do?

   1) Set off in a canoe in search of help.

   2) Build a shelter and set off in the jungle for food.

   3) Build a fire and stay at the beach.

            A) ___

            B) ___

            C) ___

            D) ___

            E) ___

F) ___

G) ___

H) ___

I) ___

J) ___

TOTAL _____

This test should by no means be considered accurate, but is a generalization about how willing you are to accept change in your life. The more questions there are, the more accurate the test.

If you scored 5—8, change is very important to you. You can't seem to tolerate the waiting game, the limits put on you, the hesitations, during periods of transition. You are not afraid of a major life change, as you always thrive on moving ahead. It's too bad for others if they can't keep up, you're moving forward. The novelty of changing quickly can bring with it instability, which can wear you out. At this point, you should stand still and ask yourself if you are confronting your problem or running away from it.

If you scored 9—12, you have a slight desire for change but see no need to act before you are required to. You feel quite content with where you are in life. You have a calm manner with a good self-image. Rather than undertaking extreme changes, you pride yourself on making the small ones to make things work. Stability is key for you.

If you scored 13—15, change is a useful and understandable step. You may not be completely satisfied with the way your life has turned out. Instead of becoming a completely new person, you would rather work on improving yourself. Personal development at a nice, even pace continually occupies your mind. You enjoy the balance in your life and avoid anything that would disrupt this harmony. When change becomes necessary in your life, you will need to address it, even if it means giving up some of those security strings that have kept everything intact.

The only person you are destined to become is the person you decide to be.

Ralph Waldo Emerson

13

From Then to Here to There

At what point should we begin with "then"? The invention of the wheel started things rolling (I know, but I just had to say it). The creation of fire for warmth and food preparation or carrying water in a container would seem simple acts. Today these discoveries seem pretty mundane, but imagine how amazing each was at the time. The visionaries who discovered these things, through their imagination, tremendously improved life for humankind.

TO HERE

We are fortunate to be living in an age characterized by an amazing amount of convenience, health care, and quality of life. We enjoy all of these things today because of people with vision, with imagination. Louis Pasteur created vaccines for rabies and cholera. William Morton created anesthesia (ouch). The Wright Brothers, of course, invented the airplane, but did you know that Frank Whittle invented the jet engine? Songwriters like George Gershwin and John Lennon created songs that will last generation after generation. The list goes on and is as long as it is amazing.

Who would have thought we could create a machine that would fly men to the moon and return them safely to earth? Who would have thought the amount of information stored on a computer as big as a room could now be stored on the head of a pin?

The inventions of the phone, television, and internet have all pushed the communication factor to a phenomenal level. The Scotts were the first family in my neighborhood to have a television. It was a black-and-white sixteen-inch box. Color television was still a few years away. Every Saturday morning, all of the neighborhood kids were invited over to watch the serials of superheroes. Each week, we were left wondering if our hero survived. We had to wait until the following week to find out. Our imaginations ran wild all through the week. (This meeting of the kids every Saturday continued for four weeks, until little Davy carved his initials in Mrs. Scott's coffee table!)

Today, almost everyone has a cell phone and a computer. With the use of satellites floating high above the earth, we can talk to anyone with a phone half the size of our hands from almost anywhere. Live video traveling from the other side of the planet into our computers and televisions is just an accepted way of life.

TO THERE

"To there" is the rest of your life. I am not suggesting that you reinvent the wheel, create a new fuel source, or find a cure for cancer. You and only you are responsible for how you harness your thoughts, your imagination. We each are an entity unto ourselves. How many thoughts do you keep to yourself in a day? How many different thoughts have

only you are responsible for how you harness your thoughts

you had in the past hour? How random is your mind? Are your thoughts all sequential and organized or are they all over the place? It's amazing when you think about it. It would probably be an accurate estimate to say that 90 percent of these thoughts are never shared with anyone else. This means you are the sole proprietor of your thoughts for the rest of your life, which gives you free rein to shape, nurture, and hone your imagination to create what you desire.

*Habit is the best of servants,
or the worst of masters.*

Nathaniel Emmons

14

Habits

The preceding quote says it all. You can benefit from your habits or they can be your downfall. You want to be the best that you can be. An action that you do repeatedly, whether positive or negative, eventually becomes involuntary. You don't even think about it. As a result, your logic has no say in what you are doing and doesn't really register until after the behavior. This is why we do things we know we shouldn't do. Later we may regret what we have done. Once you realize that life is a series of habits, both good and bad, you can work on controlling those habits to improve your life. If a habit is a learned behavior, then with a concentrated effort, it can be eradicated. Breaking a habit can be very difficult, but you know you can do it.

a repeated behavior eventually becomes a habit

Yesterday, you did several things that were habits. Recall yesterday in your mind. Now that you have thought about the day, write down one action that you thought was a bad habit and one action that you thought was good. Be honest with yourself; no one is looking over your shoulder. Now imagine just how much your life would improve by eliminating one negative habit and adding one positive one.

To eliminate a negative habit or establish a positive one requires that you take control of your gratification. Make gratification work for you by receiving it for accomplishing your immediate goal. I have stopped eating late at night. I have quit smoking. I get up on time for work. I feel good about these new behaviors. When your gratification for eliminating a habit or establishing a new one exceeds the pleasure you felt engaging in your previous behavior, you are well on your way to taking control of your habits. Make instant gratification work for you instead of against you.

*A kind and compassionate
act is often its own reward.*

William John Bennett

15

Giving Builds Character and Confidence

People of character, people of confidence, all give back in some way, whether it be in money, possessions, or service. When helping others along your journey to success, you are not only enhancing your strength of character but developing your self-confidence as well. What, you say, developing your self-confidence, how can that be? You need to look no further than your own

> **It feels Good Doing For others**

experience. Recall the last time you gave of yourself. It may be a simple thing, such as opening a door for a stranger, dropping a coin in an open hat, or letting a car get in front of you during rush hour. Now recall the emotion, the feeling that went with that action. It felt good, didn't it? Doing for others feels good. Your confidence increases along with your motivation to achieve what you are striving for. It comes right around back to you.

No one would disagree that giving makes the world a better place. When you give of yourself, whether it be monetary or in service, you will immediately begin to feel the personal benefits.

One of the best things you can do for yourself is to give to others. The power of giving will make you happy and help lead you to your own personal success. You would think that the status of a person's income would determine whether that person gives away a portion of his or her money. This is not necessarily so. Low-income people still give to others in need. The act of giving is not just for Bill Gates and Warren Buffet.

In a recent study, MRI scans showed an increased amount of activity in the *nucleus accumbens* and *caudate nucleus* areas of the brains of people making financial donations. These two areas of the brain have been associated with the brain's response to a rewarding, or "feel-good," stimulus. Another study found that donating money activated the part of the brain associated with money, food, sex, and drugs. It just feels good to give or to help someone else.

There is reason to give besides the "feel-good" response. One of the most successful ways of overcoming stress, negative emotions, or even depression is doing something to help someone else. When you are offering kindness, benevolence, and compassion to someone, these positive emotions override the negative emotions. When you feel good about taking a positive action, you will tend to do more good. Now that's a positive cycle everyone should experience.

List ten things that you have done for someone else in the past five days:

1. _____

2. _____

3. _____

4. _____

5. _____

6. _____

7. _____

8. _____

9. _____

10. _____

The giving of yourself, your time, or your money in an unsolicited way, whether it be for a friend, a relative, a colleague, or even a stranger, creates a feel-good response in your brain. As you wrote down the ten actions, there was joy in your heart and maybe a slight smile on your face.

Gratitude is not only the greatest of virtues, but the parent of all others.

Cicero

16

Gratitude

Do you sometimes feel that you are doing all the right things to succeed in life, taking the right courses, reading the right books, and listening to the motivational and success tapes? You do everything to succeed, but something seems to be missing. The busy lifestyle of hustling to get ahead can sometimes have us stepping on this most important component.

There are a variety of reasons why some people succeed in life while others continually fail. When you do everything you are supposed to do but do not get to where you want to be, you may ask yourself, *What am I missing? What have I left out?*

> **gratitude is a high vibration of thought**

The answer is gratitude. Your emotions, your thoughts, the energy that you put out, positive or negative, will eventually come back into your life. It's the law of attraction working.

When you are grateful for something, it is a very powerful energy. Gratitude creates a high "vibration" of thought, which comes back to you through the law of attraction. In this book, when I am talking about you achieving your idea, I emphasize visualizing yourself at your goal. This gives you an immediate sense of well-being because you are grateful for being at your goal. Remember, there must be some present feeling of well-being, of being grateful. It helps you to continue putting high energy into your project. You are exercising gratitude.

In the past, you may have thought of being grateful as just a state of mind in reaction to a part of your life. Gratitude is actually one of the tools in your mindset to achieve the life you want. When you are grateful, you want to give. When you give, you will receive.

List ten things in your life for which you are grateful:

1. _____

2. _____

3. _____

4. _____

5. _____

6. _____

7. _____

8. _____

9. _____

10. _____

Now that you have listed ten things for which you are grateful, you have at least exercised the feeling of gratitude in the brain—but will it sustain itself? Gratitude is much like motivation, for it must come from within to be longlasting rather than a temporary fix.

The sorcery and charm of imagination and the power it gives the individual to transform his world, makes it one of the most treasured of all human capacities.

Frank Baron

17

Developing Your Imagination

Every one of us is born with this gift of imagination. The first year or so of our lives we do not really exercise it, as it is directly related in part to our life experience. As we develop, so does our imagination pool. We begin to engage in fantastic childhood fantasies of flying like Superman and taking on superhero roles. It seems that anything is possible.

Our world of "pretend" then begins to dwindle as we mature. It is no longer acceptable to daydream or fantasize about things that could be. We gradually fall into a rut of thinking the same kinds of thoughts, creating the same images. We do it in an almost automatic fashion. We become set in our ways and our thoughts, which turn into either positive or negative habits. Imagination is thought, and thought creates our future reality.

thought creates our future reality

We all have the fantastic ability to use our imaginations to travel anywhere, do anything, or be anybody. Doing so does not cost a dime and does not hurt or bother another individual. We are born with this ability. We have never had to work at it because it comes so naturally. The creative imagination that we are all born with sets us apart from, and ahead of, all other living things on this earth. A bear eats all summer to gain the weight to sustain it through the winter. A humming bird gains twice its weight for its long flight south across the Gulf of Mexico for the winter. We call these actions "instincts," which are not taught but are survival mechanisms built into the species. As humans, we have a built-in creative mechanism that allows us to form a variety of goals and alter them at will.

THE POSSIBILITIES ARE INFINITE

We can all use this creative imagination to achieve our goals, in both our personal and professional lives. Imagining, thinking, daydreaming, or whatever you want to call it, is constructive only if you act upon it. When you do not take action, your imagination is just present-time fantasy enjoyment. Most people are waiting for their ships to come in when they haven't sent one out or moved to action on what they thought about.

You should not forget to exercise your imagination, as it thrives on workout. Here is some "food for thought." Play with these for a while; then add a few of your own:

- What would you do if you could fly?

- What would you do if you had enough money that you never had to work again?

- What would you do with your life if you were immortal?

- What three foods would you like if stranded on an island?

- If you could be any animal, what would you be?

- Which superhero would you be: Spiderman, Batman, or Superman?

- What would you do if you couldn't fail?

- What brings a smile to your face?

- What is your version of success?

- What does being a hero mean to you?

People forget how fast you did a job, but they remember how well you did it.

Howard W. Newton

18

Efficiency

It is no revelation that essentials for success in any endeavor include efficiency and organization. Our entire existence, both our work and our pleasure, is the result of organization. All of the things we do are planned or arranged. Why would people tolerate, as so many do, inefficiency in themselves, especially when they can do something about it? Successful people plan and organize, and are more efficient than others are.

> successful
> people
> plan and
> organize more
> efficiently

The fact that you have picked this book up now and are reading it is a positive move toward organization. You are now becoming a doer instead of a wisher. You want to improve yourself. You are taking action. You are becoming more efficient. The organization of your time, your priorities, your chores, your pleasures allows you to lead a more fulfilling life.

Efficiency in the workplace has always been a concern in the corporate world. A basic salary paid without any kind of incentive encourages employees to do the minimum required work. A few airlines have now brought in employee shares; efficiency has gone up, as has the value of the shares. Fringe benefits, whether they be time off, discounts, or free merchandise, create happy employees and greater efficiency.

To listen well, is as powerful a means of influence as to talk well, and is essential to all true conversation.

Chinese Proverb

19

Listening

One of the most crucial aspects to success in any area of your life is communication. You have communicated, and will continue to communicate, throughout your entire existence. How well you can communicate will have a direct influence on your ability to achieve success, realize your goals, and establish desired relationships with others. Why do so many people have difficulty with this skill? The most crucial factor in communication is listening.

Think right now of all the people in your life you talk to everyday: friends, family, business colleagues and clients. As you recall each person, ask yourself, *Is he or she a good listener?* Are there people who never seem to be listening to you because they are thinking of what they want to say? Do you get the annoying feeling that what you have to say isn't as important to them? This is the result when you are on the receiving end of a bad listener. This can be crucial to a relationship or business opportunity.

opportunities are missed because of poor listening skills

Many people have missed opportunities by not listening to what the other side had to say. One of the classic episodes from the *Seinfeld* sitcom was Kramer suing the coffee company when he spilled hot coffee on himself. The company had decided to offer Kramer a lifetime supply of coffee and $50,000. Kramer entered the office. The company president said, "We would like to settle with you and are willing to give you a lifetime supply of coffee and …" "I'll take it!" screamed Kramer before the president could offer the money.

Most people appreciate and are drawn to a person with good listening skills. They feel like this person is interested in what they have to say. Quite often, prospective clients will reveal, and enjoy talking about, much more than they were asked if they feel there is genuine interest. People like to tell you what they know, which can be quite revealing.

If you want others to be happy, practice compassion. If you want to be happy, practice compassion.

Dalai Lama

20

Happiness

An emotion we all seek but not everyone attains is happiness. What happiness means to one person can be quite different from what it means to another. It is an emotion associated with joy, bliss, satisfaction, and contentment. It may exist in parts of your life or in all of your life. When your thinking is pleasant and contented most of the time, you are happy.

When you are happy, when you can laugh, when you think pleasant thoughts, every part of your body functions more efficiently. Modern medicine has proven that all of our internal organs—the stomach, the liver, and even the heart—perform better when we are happy. The senses become more keen and aware. Research has shown that eyesight actually improves when a person visualizes pleasant thoughts.

our body functions more efficiently when we are happy

PURSUING HAPPINESS

One of the major obstacles in the pursuit of happiness is the "waiting-for-the-future-to-happen" syndrome. Unhappy people do not live in or enjoy the present because they are waiting for the future. I will be happy when I graduate, when I get a better paying job, when I get a car, when I leave home, when I get married, when I pay off the mortgage, when I win the lotto. Happiness is a mental mindset, an attitude that needs to be in the present consciousness of the individual, or it may never be attained.

HAPPINESS CAN BE RELATIVE

Many people today are obsessed with status to the point that it is the underlying factor in their unhappiness. How are you living relative to those around you? When you hang with millionaires and you are not one, it will be a constant battle to keep up. When you own the cheapest house on the street, it may be a good financial investment regarding resale, but living in it may bring on that status anxiety. Choose your neighborhood and your peers wisely to avoid any diminishment in your happiness.

THINK HAPPY

You are completely responsible for your own thoughts. It's what you think about and your resulting attitudes that create happiness. We all go along on a psychological plane that constantly fluctuates around the line that separates the positive from the negative. It's how we decide to react to this multitude of circumstances that helps determine our level of happiness. The friend that you were going to meet for lunch is late, you were slow advancing your car when the light turned green and the person behind you honked the horn, the plane to make your connection is late in

your resulting attitude will create happiness

boarding. These everyday events can make us exhibit feelings of resentment, anger, and self-pity, which of course replace the emotion of happiness. It's all about attitude, which is always your choice.

THE FIX TO HAPPINESS

People quite often seek happiness through the quick fixes of medication, coffee, and fatty foods. You may find a spending splurge on clothes, electronics, or a new car does the deed. Remodeling the house, attending a movie, or taking a vacation can also bring happiness. These purchases are temporary bandages and lack the true ingredient to keep you happy. After a short while, you will return to your previous level of happiness. To have depth and meaning to your life, to be contented and satisfied will require happiness that comes from within and is long lasting. A person is happiest when working toward a goal.

Often, we realize how much a relationship has meant to us only after we have lost the loved one. Why wait until it is too late? Do not let the permanence of death jolt you into that "if only I had" stage. Do it now, call that person, reestablish that relationship. Good relationships are the glue of true happiness. Make them a priority in your life.

All the wonders of the world created by man pale in comparison to man himself.

Robert Mesmer

21

Your Automatic Success Mechanism

All the wonders of the world created by man pale in comparison to man himself. It seems almost ironic that, when born, man is one of the most helpless creatures on this earth. Yet, in a few short years, we rise to the other end of the scale as the most dominant. It's more than just brain matter, but a combination of our brains and automatic nervous systems working together to create ideas and visions.

When you are hot, you perspire. The evaporation of your perspiration cools the body. You do not think about this; it happens automatically. The automatic nervous system runs continually, whether you are asleep or awake. It is designed to control sudden activity when required, such as your blood pressure, your heart rate, your glucose production, and even the dilation of your pupils. It can also react in a calming manner by bringing blood pressure and heart rate down to a more relaxed and healthier level.

Your brain and nervous system work together to achieve a certain goal, solve a problem, or create a new idea or vision. This combination functions automatically to point you in the right direction and even to make adjustments as required. How you perceive yourself and your vision is the major contributing factor as to whether this is a "success" or "failure" mechanism. When you swing at a pitched ball, your brain gives the signal, but you can't possibly know which muscles to use and in what combination. You just swing at the ball. It's automatic. Your brain working in combination with your nervous system, sends the signals to the muscles and, through experience, corrects and adjusts almost instantly. This automatic mechanism receives data,which the brain has obtained through the eyes, that on the next pitch the bat should be held in a higher position.

how you perceive yourself helps decide success or failure

You have already been using this process for years. Tying your shoelace or riding a bike is evidence that you have made the correct adjustments to succeed. As you adjusted, you remembered a correct response and forgot an incorrect one. You can apply this automatic success system again and again to any area of your life, because you already have the process.

You cannot be lonely if you like the person you're alone with.

Dr. Wayne Dyer

22

Self-Image

How you perceive yourself, your self-image, is key in reprogramming or even maintaining the person you want to be. Your self-image is where you look to tell yourself how to behave or react to any situation. When you feel inferior, the ability to act in a confident manner is much more difficult. The vision you may have been carrying with you for years may be holding you back.

> it is up to you to create a positive self image

The subconscious mind believes whatever it receives. The person who sends it pictures and images of inadequacy or doubt is surely doomed to failure. You will want to create positive, successful visual messages to your subconscious. Your subconscious automatically coordinates your thoughts and behavior to achieve your desired goal. The recurring theme throughout this book is "you become what you think about." It is up to you to control and create these positive self-images of yourself as you want to be.

23

Self-Esteem

How you feel about yourself affects the way other people feel about you. You must first like yourself if you want other people to like you. Your self-esteem controls how you think and, as a result, how you behave and make decisions. The more you like yourself, the more confident you will be to achieve your goals. The process of improving your self-esteem does not mean perfection, for that is a dead end. There is no up from perfection. There is only one place to go from perfection and that is down. Do not beat yourself up striving for perfection.

> **your self esteem effects how you make decisions**

All people, at some time in their lives, have felt that they were faking it, especially during a transition or a new experience outside of their comfort zone.

How you perceive yourself determines your self-esteem. What is your self-image? Are you assertive or timid, confident or withdrawn, attractive or dull? Self-image is an enduring personality trait that can, though normal, have short-term variations. You may have a more positive self-image temporarily when you are in your comfort zone, not being threatened by an outside stimulus.

To live in a healthy way and lead a fulfilling, happy life, it is essential that you have a positive self-esteem.

The successful person has the habit of doing the things failures don't like to do. They don't like doing them either necessarily. But their disliking is subordinated to the strength of their purpose.

E. M. Gray

24

Self-Discipline

Although discussed briefly in the chapter on success, self-discipline is a core ingredient, which merits further examination. Self-discipline is basically having control over yourself to take action to do what you should do, regardless of whether you feel like it or not. Your ability to achieve is unlimited when you can commit yourself to follow through on your best

> self-discipline will empower you

intentions no matter what the circumstances. You can lose the weight you want, exercise and train, study and read the hours required, keep your house, office, and garage in the orderly fashion you desire; the possibilities are endless. You will know when you are completely in charge of your discipline when you make a conscious decision and you are sure that you will follow through on it. Self-discipline will empower you to take risks, make decisions, and overcome anything in your way. There is no procrastination, disorder, or ignorance when you exercise self-discipline.

Robert Mesmer

ROOM FOR IMPROVEMENT

Just as each one of us is a unique individual, so is our level of self-discipline. The more disciplined you are, the greater the potential of your reaching your desired goal. You will want to progress at building this discipline, just like anything else, a little bit at a time. When you train for a marathon, you might begin with a few miles a day. You begin slowly and gradually increase your daily training miles. It is the same thing with training yourself in a discipline. As you carry out an action, you receive immediate gratification, which then will spur you on to challenge yourself. It doesn't matter how much discipline you have now, it's what you will have tomorrow and the next day. You are comparing yourself to you and not to others. You will now see progress.

A former student of mine called me one day and asked if I would meet with him. He was a draftsman in the government. He was responsible for the legal survey of individual lots being added to the master plan. He had been with the government seven years and done all the courses, was always on time, and never missed a day of work. He was continually being passed over for promotions to the next level. His supervisor had told him that the quality of his work was good, but his production was average. I asked him to describe his day to me. He shared a room with five other draftsmen. He said they were all great to work with; while they worked, they talked all day about sports and their weekends. On occasion, their breaks would run a little long if they got into a good discussion, but it was all in fun and they all got along well. I told him he had two choices: continue to enjoy his routines and stay in that job forever, or look seriously at his time management and try to improve it. The first step would be to limit his breaks to the allotted break time. Step two, again a small but positive step, would be to focus just on his work for the first hour of each day. In the third step, he should do the same during the first hour of the afternoon. This required a gradual building of self-discipline. He was promoted the following year.

DEVELOPING SELF-DISCIPLINE

The first thing you must do to develop discipline is to throw out any attitude of denial. You could be in denial because you are not facing reality; as far as you are concerned, everything is fine. When you are trying to accomplish something and your wheels are spinning, look at yourself honestly. What are you doing that you could improve upon and make a new habit? This is very difficult for most people, so let me give you some examples and as you read them, a little voice should be sounding off in your mind. *Yep, that's me I guess, oh, and that ...and that, I could change that.*

> being in denial of a bad habit is not facing reality

Hygiene—Do you brush your teeth every morning and before bed? Do you bathe everyday? Eating—Are you overweight? Do you eat a lot of fast food? Time Management—Do you get up on time for work? Do you allow yourself enough sleep time? Do you watch TV more than two hours a day? Do you feel you waste time during the day? Breaking addictions—alcohol, caffeine, salt, sugar—requires self-discipline. Office: Is your computer scattered with files all over the desktop? Is your inbox beginning to fill up? Goals: Do you set goals? Do you write down goals? Do you reach all your goals? Face whatever reality is in your life and change it. You are in control of your life and will be amazed at the results when you organize self-disciplines and adhere to them one at a time, day by day.

When you understand gratification and how to deal with it, you will be well on your way to having self-discipline in any area of your life. The problem with most people is that they have conditioned themselves to require instant gratification for everything they do and want. As a baby, you expected instant gratification:"I want my bottle and I want it now!" As you develop, you learn to put off this instant reward for a more important future goal. When you have difficulty with this concept, you want it now, you overextend your credit card to have that iPod or trip now. You have that smoke, that drink, or that piece of chocolate because you want it now. You stay in bed that extra twenty minutes because it's comfortable now. You stay up too late at night because you are enjoying now, not thinking of tomorrow and that you will need to be rested to perform your job efficiently.

Just like habit, immediate gratification can be the best of servants or the worst of masters. You can take your gratification mindset and turn it around in your favor. In chapter 2, Setting Successful Goals, I stress backing up from the major goal and setting smaller, immediate goals. The accomplishment of even the smallest goal will bring you immediate gratification because you realize you are taking action toward your main idea. Now, every time you reach a goal in the present, you get a positive feeling of gratification, which soon becomes habit. I did not go over my budget; I feel good about that. I got up in time for work; I feel good. I did not take that drink; I am proud of myself. You are now using gratification to establish a positive habit or eliminate a negative habit by exercising self-discipline.

Motivation is a fire from within.
If someone else tries to light that
fire underneath you, chances
are it will burn very briefly.

Steven R. Covey

25

Motivation

Are you trying to achieve a goal but feel something is holding you back? You feel you have the motivation, but something is just not clicking, putting you in gear to get there. Take another look at your motivation. While desire is an important part of motivation, it is not the determining factor in achievement. Success in reaching your goal is determined by action. You can determine your level of motivation by how much action you have taken. Do you remember when you first

determine your level of motivation by how much action you've taken

started working on a project, how confident and excited you were about moving your motivation to act into reality? Then other things in your life slowly came back into play, wearing away your enthusiasm for your idea. You started to focus on other jobs completely unrelated to your project. This is an indication that your motivation is coming from external sources rather than from within.

You may find it difficult to stay motivated if you are in college because that is what your parents wanted for you. You may be there and even get the promised carrot, but the motivation that comes from within really makes the difference. Are you in a job right now that you don't enjoy or feel any enthusiasm for, or for which you have no motivation to excel? Interest is an important motivator for anyone, as is a desire to learn. Add interest and desire and you will create success. Quite often, when you have a taste of success, it creates self-confidence and an interest and desire to learn more. You are now creating your own upward spiral of motivation to achieve your goal.

Motivation in the workplace should always be a concern of administration for management in creating an atmosphere conducive to solid performance and achievement. Here are the top ten motivators for staff that will encourage high morale, enthusiasm, and production.

1. **Give performance incentives**. These Promise employees that the more proficient and productive they are, the more they will make. You will eliminate the attitude of *just doing my job because I don't get any more for extra effort.* The incentives can come in many forms: bonuses for reaching sales quotas or beyond or even shares in the company itself. Two airlines have offered the latter to their employees and they are doing extremely well. When employee shareholders earn more for the company, they earn more for themselves as their shares become more valuable and pay higher dividends. It's now their own company.

2. **Recognize achievement**. Everyone likes to be appreciated and recognized for a job well done. This can be on an individual or group basis. The idea that the boss is aware of an employee's work is an incentive.

3. **Create opportunities**. It is very difficult to create hope, enthusiasm, and willingness to go the extra mile when there is no place to advance in a company. Hard work should pay off and the incentive doesn't necessarily need to be in monetary bonuses. The opportunity to receive company product (a winery gives a case of wine to each employee every month), or time off, or even business trips, will build morale.

4. **Show kindness**. It's such an easy thing to do. Sincerity and kindness to an employee will always go a long way toward ensuring harmony in the workplace. People who like and respect their bosses will work for them. If you bully your employees, their work ethic will go down the drain with your relationship.

5. **Create challenge**. When people are working toward a common goal, they are much happier. The job with no challenge can become very mundane. Give them a difficult problem that they can solve and feel an intrinsic reward, and they will be much more enthusiastic.

6. **Explain consequences**. The boss who threatens will not get the results he or she wants. Make the employees aware of the possibilities of what could happen if a particular job is not completed. The explanation of a situation allows the employees to own a part of it.

7. **Give detailed instructions**. Most people work much more efficiently when they know exactly what is expected of them or what job they are to complete. Give specific instructions and you will get specific results.

8. **Develop team spirit**. There is no law that says there can't be fun in the work place. An environment of camaraderie,

of team spirit, can work wonders. When people feel they are part of a team, they feel like they belong. They don't want to let the other team members down.

9. **Schedule mini-deadlines.** Set up a series of mini-deadlines leading up to a major one. Most people are more productive just before a major deadline. The deadline gives them direction and focus.

10. **Communicate.** Many individuals who have reached a supervisory position may have developed few or no people skills along the way. Communication in the workforce is paramount to success. Being aware of potential problems between employees or inconsistencies in their job descriptions will allow the company to remedy situations before they become bigger problems.

As with all motivation, the tangible carrots of shares, bonuses, dividends, and goods are the most immediate but not necessarily the longest lasting. These incentives can soon become the norm as the novelty wears off. The intrinsic reward of doing something well, of excelling toward a goal is the most durable of motivational drives.

What lies behind us and what lies ahead of us are tiny matters compared to what lies within us.

Ralph Waldo Emerson

26

Create A New
Mental Image

You will not achieve the goal of creating a new mental image of yourself with simple willpower and effort. There must be some underlying reason for you to decide that the present image is just not cutting it. The new image should be truthful and appropriate. When people do finally change their self-image, they feel they have realized the truth about themselves. The saying "the truth can set you free" is paramount in ridding yourself of an inadequate self-image.

A movie classic dealing with self-image is *To Sir with Love* starring Sidney Poitier. He played a young teacher thrust into a class of raunchy high school students who had little self-esteem or respect for each other. Although it was Hollywood theater, the theme of changing the way you thought about yourself and others was accurate. "Sir," as he was affectionately known in the movie, established a sense of purpose in his students, and made them believe that they, too, could have success in their lives.

PERSONAL GROWTH vs. SELF-ACCEPTANCE

Personal growth and self-acceptance might seem mutually exclusive at first—if you just accept the way you are, then how are you supposed to grow as an individual? It seems to go against your efforts at improving yourself. But the building of anything of substance requires a good foundation. Real self-acceptance gives you a solid base upon which to build yourself into what you

self acceptance gives a solid base to build your self image

want to become. You know and accept your faults while remembering your attributes. You now have clarity about what needs to be improved. You define yourself by your values and not by the ever-changing external things in your life, such as money, jobs, and possessions.

There is a boundary to men's passions when they act from feelings; but none when they are under the influence of imagination.

Edmund Burke

27

Imagination Rehearsal

The imaginary rehearsal of a desired outcome is not harmful to anyone and occurs completely in your own mind. It's a trip with unlimited potential. You can go anywhere, do anything, or be anybody. You have no explaining to do, and do not have to answer to anyone.

At this point, you have selected a particular goal, situation, or behavior you wish for yourself. Now, take one step back and go through this created image as a "third" person. You are now looking at this image as the creator or the director, but as a bystander.

> look at
> at your
> imaginary
> rehearsal as
> a third person

As you watch this stand-in for you, watch how he/she behaves. Put everything into your image: the voice, the body language, the apparel, the physical setting. The more specific you can be, the better. Is this person performing exactly how you imagined? If not, alter something: delete a detail, add a detail, polish the rehearsal. You want to keep running through this imaginary experience until you see it unfold exactly as you desire.

The use of our imaginations gives us the opportunity to practice new attitudes and traits that we couldn't practice otherwise. This imagery is a powerful tool. There is a classic study of three groups of basketball players. At the beginning of the week, all players were tested on shooting baskets from the free-throw line. The scores were recorded and then the players were divided into three groups. In group one, each player shot one hundred baskets a day for a week. In group two, each player, without the use of a ball, imagined one hundred shots a day for a week, with the vision of each ball going through the hoop. In group three, the players practiced each day but did not shoot baskets. At the end of the week, all three groups were tested once again on shooting. Group one had the biggest percentage improvement, but group two, who had just used their imaginations, was a very close second. In group three, there was no significant change.

*You may have a fresh start
any moment you choose,
for this thing that we call
"failure" is not the falling
down, but the staying down.*

Mary Pickford

28

Top Ten Sales Attributes

Every one of us is a salesperson. Everyone, on occasion, is trying to convince another to do, act, believe, or agree on something. You started as an infant announcing that you were hungry and it was time to eat by letting out a cry. As you grew older, your actions, one hopes, became more sophisticated. You may be trying to convince your friends to see a particular movie or your spouse to buy a particular car. You may be in the persuasion market professionally as a consultant, administrator, or sales representative. It is the stuff of our lives' interactions. Some of us are more persuasive than others, but it is a skill that can be learned. The most successful persuaders are the people who have developed these skills effectively. The following information is not new or guarded in secret by the privileged few. However, if you took the top one hundred salespeople in the world and did a cross-reference of success traits, they would possess these attributes.

> everyone of us is a salesperson

1. **Self-confidence**. You must have a belief in yourself and in your idea or product. There is a too-common attitude

that a person can sell without having the sincerity that he or she has a good product. It can be a very difficult thing to do to believe that you are the best and that you are capable of being a consistent high achiever. We all have that inner voice asking us if we are for real or just fakes that no one has yet discovered. Self-confidence can silence that voice as dominant thoughts of positive images occupy the mind, leaving little room for self-doubt.

2. **Association with the right people.** You want to hang with people who are successful and have a positive "can-do" attitude. Think of all the people you know. How many of them continually come up with excuses and always seem to have a negative opinion about everything. They whine, they complain, but they never take any real action. These attitudes of disenchantment should be left in their court, not yours. When you associate with them, you become them. Surround yourself with positive, supportive people and you will become an achiever.

3. **Knowledge of the product.** Your prospects want and expect not just facts, but answers, from you. You owe it to your customers to have the latest information and know how it affects them in the use of your product. The top salespeople in the world are the first to admit they never stop learning.

4. **Recognizing opportunity and jumping on it.** Negative people quite often have opportunity standing right in front of them, staring them in the face. They cannot see the opportunity because of their attitude. A positive attitude is the breeding ground of imagination, which leads to action, which leads to achievement in sales. Look at the menus of McDonald's or Red Robin to see how they have catered to the cuisine imaginations of the younger age groups.

5. **Willingness to take risk and make mistakes.** One of the most important attributes of success in sales is to be able to step forward and take a risk or make a mistake. Great opportunities and accomplishments have been born of mistakes. Don't think of a failure as a mistake, but as a learning experience that you won't repeat. You are one further step toward success with every failure. The readiness to take a chance is a common attribute among successful salespeople. That chance is less risky the more you prepare and educate yourself. This preparation in itself creates the self-confidence to take the chance or risk. You need to ask yourself if you are willing to risk whatever it takes to get you to your goal or close your sale.

6. **A positive attitude.** How many people do you know who are deep into their careers and tainted with irreversible cynicism? You probably know a few, as we all do. In some vocations, negative people may be able to function, but certainly do not look forward to going to work each day. In sales, cynicism is a deadly sin. People want to do business with people they like. No one enjoys being with a negative person. It just isn't fun.

7. **Staying focused on the goal.** People who succeed in sales do not let distractions move them off course. Many diversions will pop up along the path. It is completely up to those people as to how they react to these side streets. The mind set to stay on course and follow the dream will turn that dream into reality.

8. **Taking responsibility.** When you are successful, you take responsibility for everything you do. You realize that everything that happens to you is a result of your actions. You do not blame other people. You wouldn't waste time on petty blame, even though at times it would be just as

easy to blame someone else. Instead of passing the blame, successful people move on and get the job done.

9. **Never giving up.** Success comes with perseverance. The people that fail usually do so because they quit too soon. The people that succeed continue to move ahead even when encountering seemingly impossible odds. If you want to be a success, make a plan, set some short-term and long-term goals, and stick to them. Whether it be in your personal or professional life, in sales or any form of work, the person who wants it the most and doesn't give up will get the pie.

10. **Taking action.** A dream is just a fantasy. A dream with action becomes a reality. "Let's move on it"; "Go for it"; "Just do it" are the expressions kick-starting the actions that lead to success. I was sitting in the airport waiting for my connection, talking to a gentleman in his mid-forties. He told me he had seen *The Secret* and had pictured his dream home, visualized it, thought about it, but nothing ever happened to him. I asked him what actions he had taken toward getting his new house. *The Secret* didn't work for him because he failed to move, to take action beyond his dream, or in this case, fantasy.

These ten attributes of successful salespeople are straightforward everyday characteristics. There is nothing new here. Achievers have had these qualities for years. Why are they so difficult to master for so many people? It all comes down to discipline. If you are not willing to exercise the disciplines that will bring you to success, then you don't want it badly enough. The biggest obstacle to success is you.

Does thou love life? Then do not squander time, for that is the stuff life is made of.

Benjamin Franklin

29

Time

The one constant in your life is time. We are all born with it. You can't store, inherit, or lend it. The day contains twenty-four hours, and the hour, sixty minutes, no matter who is using it. It doesn't matter who you know or how rich you are. Time is a constant. It does not hesitate or stop for anyone.

The only way to save time is to use it wisely. When you use time wisely, you invest in yourself to be a better, more efficient person in both your personal and professional life. The busiest person seems to have time for everything. A busy person does not let the chores mount up. The jobs are accomplished one after another because of organization. To the busy person, time is too valuable a commodity to handle wastefully or without thought. If you have no time for anything, you might want to reassess your time-management skills.

> **when you use time wisely you invest in yourself**

TIME AND PROCRASTINATION

Do you know someone who just can't seem to come to grips with making a decision? Do they put off taking action or procrastinate? Probably the most time-consuming habit, indecision, has caused more people to miss more opportunities than any other factor. Procrastinating not only brings about financial loss but will cause you to suffer a higher level of stress as well.

A man was hired at a large chicken farm. His job was that of egg sorter. He had to sort the eggs as they came along the conveyer belt into small, medium, and large cartons. Three hours into the job, the hired man decided to quit. He was perspiring profusely and looked quite worn, as if he had been doing heavy-construction work. The supervisor asked him if the work was too hard. The hired man replied, "No, but the decisions are killing me!"

You have a choice of either making a decision or not. Most procrastination is due to the fear of making a decision. You are better off making mistakes than not making any decision at all and remaining in "decision limbo" as potential opportunities pass you by. The longer you take to make a decision, the closer you are to not making one at all. This does not mean you should not give consideration and though to your decisions. When you are wrong, you can correct your mistake and learn from it.

indecision equals missed opportunities

Do you spend too much valuable time over small decisions? Do you continually "second-guess" your decision after you have made it?

Procrastination is less likely to occur when there is immediate gratification. Do you notice that the longer the deadline you have for a project, the greater tendency you have to procrastinate? This is a phenomenon known as temporal delay. The closer you get to an achievement, the more valuable the reward seems. As a result, the less likely you are to put off the work needed to earn it. How many millions of people are and will be living in retirement poverty because the idea of saving or planning for this eventual outcome was just too far away?

You are searching for the magic key that will unlock the door to the source of power; and yet you have the key in your own hands, and you may use it the moment you learn to control your thoughts.

Napoleon Hill

30

Negative Imagination

We are constantly bombarded with positive and negative thoughts, which are, of course, visions, images stuck in our minds' eyes. When you are up to bat and someone in the stands shouts, "Easy out," you have two choices: you can begin believing that you are going to strike out and you most likely will, or you can completely ignore the comment and believe you are going to connect with this incoming pitch. Unfortunately, too many people let the first negative vision enter their minds. As I say many times throughout this book, we become what we think about. We attract our dominant thoughts.

The hypnotic power of negative imagination is evident in cases of anorexia. The young person, usually female, is completely convinced that she is overweight. You would think that getting on the scales and seeing eighty to ninety pounds, or looking in the mirror at an obviously gaunt and undernourished body would be sufficient for her to admit she is not fat. She has become so obsessed with the idea that she is fat that she is determined not to eat. The incredible power of the imagination now becomes evident.

Although all great accomplishments come from man's imagination, so do all failures. When you think of your achievements in the past, you are inspired to succeed in the future. It is much the same when you dwell on your failures. The running of these negative thoughts through your mind can limit you in motivation, self-confidence, and future achievement. Regard failures as stepping-stones to success.

failures are stepping stones to success

Everyone has failures; it's the way you respond to them that counts.

There is more to us than we know. If we can be made to see it, perhaps for the rest of our lives we will be unwilling to settle for less.

Kurt Hahn

31

Positive Picture Board

The visualization process of picturing yourself at your short- and long-term goals cannot be overemphasized. The common trait of all great leaders—inventors, people who excel in their areas—is vision. We call them "visionaries."All people, with a little forethought, can adapt this success technique to their own lives with a vision board. Many people have used this technique and found it to be a very positive organizational skill that has propelled them on to success. Now you can use it, too.

The picture board, the mind movie, or the treasure map—we called it the flowchart when writing programs for the computer—consists of images. It is a composite visual image of where you want to go with your idea and how you are going to get there. I like to call it the Positive Picture Board. You can have as many diagrams and pictures as you want. You can cut pictures

create a flow chart with pictures

from magazines related to your project. It can be detailed and very specific or general in nature, whatever works for you and your topic. The board can consist of numbers, words, pictures, in fact, anything related to the goal. As you glance at your creation, it will give you clarity. Do you see yourself performing or speaking in front of a crowd? You can easily find pictures of crowds, cut them out and add them to your board. Make sure you include a picture of yourself!

Here is a great site with free software for constructing your Positive Picture Board:

www.coolsiteweekly.com/free-mind-mapping-software-with-easy-online-tools/

Treat people as if they were what they ought to be, and you help them to become what they are capable of being.

Johann Wolfgang von Goethe

32

Walk In
Someone Else's Shoes

A lunch-hour meeting between an advertising rep and the CEO of a major electronics firm was taking place in a restaurant in New York. The rep was trying to convince the CEO of the advantages he could offer the CEO that would encourage him to switch accounts. The rep was quite impressive and seemed to be winning over his prospective client.

The restaurant was completely full, and it took five minutes before the waitress got to their table. The rep proceeded to ream out the waitress, saying that this just wasn't good enough. The CEO looked around the restaurant and saw that there were only three waitresses and twenty tables. The rep had not assessed the situation. It was not the waitress's fault, but the management's fault for being understaffed at the peak period.

As the rep carried on about the service to the waitress, the CEO felt embarrassed, for early on in his career he had worked in a restaurant. He knew the difficulties of staffing and how the

> **do unto others as you would have them do unto you**

waiters and waitresses always received the misplaced anger. The rep, who was so close to winning this client over, lost the account. People want to do business with people they like.

Something that my mother taught me at a very young age has served me well: Do unto others as you would have them do unto you. Whenever I meet someone for the first time, whether it's a person looking for a job, a new person on the job, or even someone standing on the street with a hand out, I think, *How would I like to be treated if I were that person? What has he or she gone through in life prior to meeting me?* This philosophy will serve you well in business as well. What is it that the client wants or needs? If I were that client, I'd—. Put yourself in someone else's shoes.

People become really quite remarkable when they start thinking they can do things. When they believe in themselves, they have the first secret of success.

Norman Vincent Peale

33

What You Believe Determines Your Actions

Two young men were hiking deep in the woods of Alaska. They climbed over a bluff and came face-to-face with two small bear cubs. At first, the men thought the cubs were "so cute" as they were feasting on a salmon tossed from the river. Then they heard the roar as the mother stood up from the river's bank. They were unfortunately positioned between the cubs and the mother. Slowly one of the men sat down and changed from his sandals to his runners. "What are you doing? You can't outrun a grizzly," whispered his friend. He responded, "I don't have to; I just need to outrun you!"

In a real-life dilemma, the automatic nervous system responds to a fight-or-flight situation. The fear factor charges the muscles so that lactic acid can actually fuse out of the muscle cell into the blood. This immediate process, known as anaerobic glycolysis, in which glycogen is converted into energy without the presence of oxygen, allows glycolysis to last for minutes rather than seconds, enhancing a person's ultimate performance.

There have been many accounts of the use of superhuman strength in times of need. A small plane had crashed on the highway and rolled into a water-filled ditch. Within minutes, the plane was surrounded by motorists coming to the aid of the pilot. His leg was pinned beneath the fuselage and the plane was quickly filling with water. It was apparent that the pilot would soon drown if he could not be removed. A large man went to the edge of the plane, squatted under the water, and suddenly stood up, lifting the plane and allowing the others to drag the pilot free.

This type of feat of superhuman strength is not new. What we have discovered, however, is that the same brain and nervous system that react to the environment also tell us what the environment is. The reaction to an encounter with the bear is, of course, emotional. It is, however, the thought that is derived from the outside world and evaluated by the mind that initiates the emotional reaction. We know that the bear will threaten our survival.

our thought initiates the emotion that creates the action

This creates in our minds a mental image of what is about to occur. It is the mental images that we react to.

What if the two men who came upon the bear had actually come upon a man dressed in a bear costume? They would still act according to what they perceived to be true. You act not to what is necessarily true, but to what image your mind holds. When a hypnotized person believes his legs are paralyzed, he will not be able to walk even though he is physically capable of doing so. Imagination is a powerful mind tool that when used with creative thoughts can accomplish amazing results.

Sweat plus sacrifice equals success.

Charles O. Finley

34

Comfort Zone

Why do so many people fail to get to where they really want to be in life? They never quite reach their intentions. They go through their entire lives feeling unfulfilled and unhappy. They do have excuses, though—it's the economy, it's the location, it's the timing. These factors do, of course, come into play, but the easy way out is to hold one up and say, "This is the reason I did not exceed."

The number-one reason people do not achieve success in their lives is that they fail to or are unwilling to, step outside of their comfort zones. A comfort zone is a set of behaviors and environments that you engage in without anxiety or risk. Throughout our early lives, we were guided by our parents and teachers to step outside this zone. The first day of school when mom let go of your hand. The first school dance. Your first date. Your first job. Remember how uncomfortable you were at first? You were stepping outside of your comfort zone. These mental boundaries created a sense of security. As we continue to mature and become

to achieve success step outside of your comfort zone

more responsible for our own lives, we encounter that fork in the road. It seems much easier to stay within the zone than to step out of it. Have you stayed in a dead-end job with no opportunity of advancement because you would lose that sense of security? Even though you are in a job you don't like, you are in a comfort zone.

Highly successful people frequently step outside their comfort zones to accomplish their goals. To achieve, to succeed, you must experiment with new and different behaviors and the responses that go with them. The first time you rode your bike or the first business meeting you held, you were stepping out of your comfort zone. Each time became a little easier as you became more comfortable with the situation. The understanding of this principle, that it does get better, that you do get more confident, will help spur you on to success and achievement.

Make sure you have finished speaking before your audience has finished listening.

Dorothy Sarnoff

35

Speaking In Public

Do you have any fear or apprehension about speaking to a crowd or even a group of people? If you do, you are not alone. In fact, you are in the majority. The fear of speaking (glossophobia) is considered the number one phobia, even beating out the fear of death. I have found that comparison to be a little difficult to comprehend. You are on a cliff and you have a choice. You either speak to this group or die. Which are you going to do? The idea of speaking is just thought of more often because it is a part of our life. This phobia of speaking has had many negative effects on career advancement and success in life. It is estimated that three out of four individuals suffer from this anxiety.

3 out 4 people experience speaking anxiety

Simply ignoring or avoiding this phobia will limit you greatly in achieving any kind of success in your life. I managed to avoid it all through high school and into university. As I have mentioned earlier in the book when discussing inhibitions, I was "big-time" apprehensive about speaking to a group. In my second year of university, this lifetime phobia came to an abrupt end through no choice of my own.

My first assignment as a future teacher was to attend a class and observe a professional in action. I would not be instructing, just watching, maybe helping individual students with their seatwork. I had my choice of a grade 12, grade 9, or grade 3 class. I immediately chose the grade 3 class, thinking, *This can't be too difficult.* There were twenty-three little eight-year-olds. This was a well-run and well-behaved class. I watched the teacher when she spoke to the class, making eye contact with each of them, changing her position throughout the room—using facial expressions to emphasize a point. This teacher was amazing at using her energy to keep the little ones focused. Midafternoon, while the students were quietly working away at their seats, the teacher approached me. In a very soft whisper she said to me, "I have a dentist appointment at 3:30; could you dismiss them for me at 3:00?" I immediately thought, *What have I gotten myself into?* I answered with a confident, "Sure." This was at 2:50; there were still ten minutes to go! For the next seven minutes, I went up and down the rows as they quietly did their work. The three-minute buzzer went and they started to clean up their desks as I walked to the front of the room and sat at the teacher's desk. The final buzzer went and they all sat up straight, folded their hands on their desks, and stared at me. There was complete silence. Well, here goes—"Dismissed." They all jumped up, conversations breaking out as they moved to the door. Whew, that wasn't too bad. I had just gotten my first taste of public speaking with one word and I enjoyed it.

WHY PUBLIC-SPEAKING ANXIETY?

Why should you feel nervous when speaking or doing a presentation in front of a group? What thought processes are running through your brain that initiate this nervous reaction?

Do you recognize any of the following in your thoughts? You might make a mistake and lose your place ...they won't like you ...you will be humiliated ...you will feel like a fool ...you are going to be judged, and judged unfairly ...they will think you don't know what you are talking about ...they will get bored ... they will start talking while you are talking ... they are comparing you to someone else.

You can determine with the following test the degree of your speaking phobia. Answer each question as honestly as you can to get the most accurate results. It is best if you do it all alone, unaided. You may want to photocopy it, marking the copy instead of the book. Circle a number for each question.

When you are scheduled to do an oral presentation or take part in a meeting, do you experience any of the following?

	Never	Seldom	Occasionally	Frequently	Often
1) An upset stomach	1	2	3	4	5
2) Dizziness	1	2	3	4	5
3) Blushing	1	2	3	4	5
4) Nervousness	1	2	3	4	5
5) Feelings of self-doubt	1	2	3	4	5
6) Stuttering	1	2	3	4	5
7) Quivering lips	1	2	3	4	5
8) Trembling hands	1	2	3	4	5
9) Rapid heartbeat	1	2	3	4	5
10) Increased perspiration	1	2	3	4	5
11) Feelings of uncertainty	1	2	3	4	5
12) Feeling embarrassed	1	2	3	4	5
13) Cold hands	1	2	3	4	5
14) Shaky knees	1	2	3	4	5
15) Feeling very tense	1	2	3	4	5

16) Having negative thoughts	1	2	3	4	5
17) Feelings of insecurity	1	2	3	4	5
18) Feelings of avoidance	1	2	3	4	5
19) Rushing your talk	1	2	3	4	5
20) Feeling irritable	1	2	3	4	5

Add your total. Your anxiety toward speaking in public is _____.

LOW 20—30

Your fear of public speaking is low if you scored between 20 and 30. You probably have the same tensions as the average speaker, but generally, you have the skills and confidence to do a good job. Proper preparation of material and eating and sleeping prior to speaking are your main concerns in presenting.

AVERAGE 30—70

The majority of people fall into this category. The quality of your presentation is affected by your feeling so uncomfortable and awkward. Nervousness, tension, and apprehension influence your behavior and the way you present yourself. There is a way to get out of this zone.

SEVERE 70—100

If you scored in this point range, you suffer from glossophobia, the fear of public speaking. You will go to great lengths to avoid any activity that involves standing up and making a presentation. It's extremely difficult for you to speak in front of a group. You may even recognize great opportunities that pass you by due to your anxiety. You know that to succeed, you must address this issue.

SPEAKING UP AND OVERCOMING STAGE FRIGHT

In my early postsecondary education, I attended an interesting but questionable lesson on public speaking. The professor told the class that he was going to have each one of us come up for a brief presentation and that if we followed his instructions, noone would be nervous. He said that the two emotions of being mad and being nervous were almost impossible to express at the same time. He demonstrated this interesting psychological tidbit by having each of us, one at a time, come up in front of the class and repeat this statement: *"I know a man in the ranks, and he is going to stay in the ranks! Why? I'll tell you why! Because he simply doesn't have the ability to get things done!"*

We were handed a yardstick to hold and slam down on the desk for emphasis as we screamed out the statement. It actually worked—no one was nervous. The professor concluded that the idea of always having to be mad to eliminate nervousness would not serve us in future presentations. It did, however, get all the students up to experience their first public speaking lesson.

If you have any apprehension about public speaking, you should plan a strategy to get over it. Whatever you do in life, there will come a time when you are going to have to stand up and say something, whether it's asking or answering a question, giving a presentation or a performance, or even giving directions. The following strategies will not only assist you in giving a more relaxed, professional presentation, but will also lead you to other techniques as well.

Strategy #1: Be prepared. When you are talking about something you know very little about, it can be very stressful. In the beginning, try to talk only about ideas and concepts with which you feel comfortable. If you are to give a presentation, your preparation requires that you rehearse just as a performer would.

Strategy #2: Eat properly. Prepare for your presentation just as you would for a sporting event. The philosophy of the pregame steak is long gone. You will want to eat early enough and lightly enough so that your energy is not being sapped by your digestive process. Fruit, pasta, and salads will all serve you well.

Strategy #3: Do not memorize your speech. If you try to give your memorized speech, Murphy's Law is almost certain to raise its ugly head. You will forget a word, someone or something may interrupt you for a moment, and you will stutter and stammer and lose your audience's interest as you try to regain your composure. Learn your speech in chunks. Let's presume you are talking about baseball. Break it into chunks. For example, one chunk may be equipment. Start with a visual image from the top of the head and go down to the feet. Now you have an order to follow. The hat, the jersey, the glove, the pants, and the cleats. You can, of course, be more detailed, but I am sure you get the idea. Look at each item in detail: its material, how it's made, and its purpose. You can even have a cheat sheet of single words to remind you of each chunk. If you are going to deliver a speech more than once, you can gradually eliminate the sheet. You now have a talk.

Strategy #4: Do not use cough drops. Any cough medicine with menthol should be avoided, as it dries the mouth and throat. Anything with glycerin is okay, as it lubricates the throat. Whatever you take, make sure it's gone before your presentation. There is nothing more irritating to an audience than the speaker's swishing around a candy in his or her mouth.

Strategy #5: Visualize yourself as a confident, relaxed, and polished speaker. Keep that image in your mind. Visit it everyday and often prior to your presentation. You are creating a "positive power picture." In practice, pretend that you are that person. Your audience wants to see you do well. The more relaxed you are, the more relaxed the audience will be. Now, go out and play that role in your presentation. You will be amazed at the result.

Strategy #6: Have some water on stage. You may feel fine prior to your speech, but the added stress on your throat from speaking could cause you to seize up halfway through your talk. It is acceptable to have water with you. You will want to think of your environment when deciding whether to have a glass or a bottle. Standing in formal wear and drinking out of a bottle is just not acceptable.

Strategy #7: Record your talk. One of the great tools at your disposal for improving your talk is a recording, or even better, a video of your presentation. It can be a real eye-opener and help you quickly knock off the rough edges and polish it up. View the video or listen to the audio with friends or colleagues and ask their opinion. It's the next best thing to having your own coach.

Strategy #8: Make eye contact with the audience. The more people you can include, the better. When you have made eye contact, even briefly, the audience feels involved. Do not mistake some blank faces in the audience for hostility; many people do not smile when they are concentrating.

Strategy #9: Check your timing. One of the most important things in giving a talk is timing. The biggest offenders, and we've all heard them, are the people that actually introduce the speakers. They enjoy the microphone, have gotten a couple of laughs, and don't want to give it up. You should know the length of time you have and the actual speaking time, from rehearsal, that you need.

Strategy #10: Join a Toastmasters' group. If you are really serious about developing your speaking skills, you will seek out a group in your area. People in Toastmasters' groups meet once a week with the common goal of enhancing their speaking skills. There is no cost or pressure to attend and there is probably a group that meets close to you. Google the Toastmasters to find a meeting appropriate to your schedule and location.

Carry an introduction. The master of ceremonies who has decided he likes the microphone because he has gotten a couple of laughs now goes into uncharted, unrehearsed territory with an introduction that bombs. Now you walk on and have to win the audience back. Depending on the environment you are speaking in, you may wish to have a written introduction in your pocket to give to the MC. You should have your intro typed in at least fourteen-point type. I always carry two. It's a fact of life that between the time you give it to him, and the time he goes on to introduce you, with all the excitement, he misplaces it. Having a spare copy is part of preparing for success.

36

Susan: A Case Study

I have included one case study in this book. Susan's story of success in her life and how she achieved it will be an inspiration to anyone who feels there are just too many obstacles to getting to where you want to be. I have not edited the story, but let Susan tell it in her own words. Thank you, Susan, for sharing.

I was born out of wedlock in 1946, in Hamburg, Germany. I was placed in a home for children. I was born with a disposition to dream and imagine. I always listened to people who were older and positive. My mother took me out of the home after two years, and into a negative environment. I had a fabulous grandmother, who I believe has always "sat on my shoulders throughout my life." She was the most powerful, positive influence. She would read Tarot cards and read the lines in my hands, all the while only being positive and telling me that I was going to have a positive and fabulous future, and to never lose faith in the process of life.

As a result, I was a dreamer and looked for the greatness, and curiosity of life and read and dreamed and imagined all things positive. At age nine, we immigrated to Canada, never to see my grandmother again, but always holding her in my heart and my soul. My father, who had been in a concentration camp as a non-Jew, but a political prisoner, wanted to take his children out of Germany. He was forty-four, and my mother forty-one, when they left Germany, not knowing what was on the other side, nor having the ability to speak English. As in all immigrants' lives, they had to take the jobs available to survive. This led to my having to work with them in janitorial jobs at age ten.

The stress of being immigrants weighed heavy on the family, as well as having a father who was very abusive, demanding, and tormenting to his children. My way out was to read, dream, and imagine a world that was positive. I was very lucky to see the positive in other people and was very open to learning from other people, since my family nucleus was not a positive source for learning. I learned from the negative also and found it to be a motivating force to be and to do well in life. I never ever forgot the positive voice within me that was the reflection of my grandmother and that was to look fear in the eyes, and to keep going.

Other than reading, I found my consolation in sports. I kept busy working, reading, and going ice skating at a local arena. The friends I met; their parents, and their influence was a very positive factor in my life. All that came to an end, when my parents decided to immigrate to the United States at forty-nine and forty-six respectively, taking my sister and me with them. I was fifteen and had no choice. I was uprooted again and left Canada screaming. I cried for days on end, but found my consolation in books.

I had many negative experiences that helped me realize that the only way out was to go through them and to learn from them. I worked every menial job, and thanked every person who gave me the opportunity to keep on keeping on. I worked many jobs, as well as going to school. I made new wonderful friends, and learned from their parents. I always identified with people older than myself and learned by their experiences and positive attitudes and input. One summer, I worked eighteen hours per day, seven days per week. I gave my parents their down payment to their house. Soon thereafter, I found out that my father had not been my biological father, and I suffered. As a result of my not speaking to my parents, my father helped me pack two shopping bags and threw me out on the streets. I never came back to live with them.

An Italian family, to whom I will always be grateful, took me into their home. I paid minimal rent and worked in kitchens where I could eat. I worked and lived with the Italian family for the next two years. I also babysat for officers on a police department who became my mentors. I was athletic and found many friends who strove to be their best. My friends who knew of my situation would invite me to their homes to make sure I ate, and had their families as a source for discussion of important issues. I found my mental health, and positive attitude through the sharing of my friends' parents, and in the positive direction that they gave me. I graduated from high school, and moved in behind some Marine Corps fighter pilots. They became my mentors also. I also stayed in touch with all my police officer friends who provided guidance and who never knew of my real circumstances until I was over eighteen and I was assured they would not use the system to put me in a foster home.

My teachers were also a wonderful source of positive reinforcement, as well as thepPrincipal of my high school. To this day, I am still in contact with many of them. When my U.S. Marine Corps pilots left for Vietnam, they made me promise to continue in school, and to make them proud by contributing something to the United States. By the time they returned, I was at the University of California, getting ready to go to law school in San Diego.

There also, I had fabulous professors, and a dean of the law school, that made all the difference in my life. I had many people help me, including a wonderful woman of the age of eighty, who lent me the money to go to law school. She was a homesteader from Colorado and had no children. She was much like my grandmother. She impacted my life in a great way. I never ever lost my sense of gratitude to the thousands of people that impacted my life.

Out of my gratitude came my positive attitude, and I always felt that I had to pay them back by passing on my generosity by being there for others. Gratitude has always been my motivator, as well as fear of the unknown propelling me forward toward rising to my own highest potential. I was not limited by fear and insisted on being introspective to find the way to move forward. I had to learn humility and patience in a profound way of listening to others and their perceptions. My gratitude was endless and caused me never to give up on my dreams. I went through law school, and continued to associate with intelligent people, who were not afraid to laugh at their own mistakes and learn from them.

I was a deputy district attorney when I left law school, and found my place in the sun by helping others help themselves, as others had done for me. I also was appointed to be an Assistant United States Attorney. After serving as a prosecutor for twelve years, and learning from police officers and many great people who worked in the crime lab, I ran against an incumbent judge, and won the election. I was the lesser of two evils, and thought it was incumbent upon me to better serve our community. The community agreed and I was voted into office in 1984. I served as a judge for twenty-two years. Upon being inducted, I invited all my mentors to be there at my induction so that I could say "thank you." I have never lost the dream. My gratitude was my sense of enthusiasm. I made many mistakes but learned from all of them. I learned to accept my weaknesses, as well as my strengths. It required going within my soul to reach for answers. I went to places inside of myself. Many people have a fear that won't allow them to go there. I remained thankful to all the people who shared my life; who helped me through thick and thin, and who taught me to be my own best friend. I never lost the dream.

37

Your Personal Blueprint For Success

Your personal blueprint for success can be applied to any area of your life, personal or professional.

☛ **STEP ONE.** DEFINE YOURSELF.

The following are success statements. Convert them to your life. Tick the left circle if this statement is not part of your life. Tick the middle circle if undecided. Tick the right circle if you feel strongly that this statement is a part of your life. Work at eventually moving all the ticks to the right circles. You do not have to have all of these statements in your life to be successful, but the more you have, the more equipped you will be to meet any challenge. Answer every question and be honest with yourself. Do the analysis in pencil, as you will want to erase any left and middle circles eventually.

○ ○○ 1) I add a new word to my vocabulary each week.

○ ○○ 2) I have a good vocabulary.

○ ○○ 3) I have used a vision board in working toward a goal.

○ ○○ 4) I read educational books.

○ ○○ 5) I keep a daily journal.

○ ○○ 6) I plan my day.

○ ○○ 7) I always use my time wisely.

○ ○○ 8) I have set long-term goals.

○ ○○ 9) I have set short-term goals to reach my long-term goals.

○ ○○ 10) I feel good when I complete one of my goals.

○ ○○ 11) I have achieved a long-term goal.

○ ○○ 12) I am confident in making decisions.

○ ○○ 13) I can make quick decisions.

○ ○○ 14) I do not let negative thought enter my mind.

○ ○○ 15) I make my dominant thoughts positive ones.

○ ○○ 16) I have good self-discipline.

○ ○○ 17) I listen to people when they are talking to me.

○ ○○ 18) I have a good sense of humor most of the time.

○ ○○ 19) I have a good memory.

○ ○○ 20) I have succeeded in at least ten things in my life.

○ ○○ 21) I do crossword puzzles.

○ ○○ 22) I can visualize situations quite easily.

○ ○○ 23) I exercise my imagination in a positive way.

○ ○○ 24) I have volunteered for at least five things in my life.

○ ○○ 25) I belong to a club or organization.

○ ○○ 26) I have moved out of my comfort zone to achieve.

○ ○○ 27) I have organized thoughts most of the time.

○ ○○ 28) I can identify a bad habit if I have one.

○ ○○ 29) I know that I can eradicate a bad habit.

○ ○○ 30) I can identify my good habits.

○ ○○ 31) I can establish a good habit if needed.

○ ○○ 32) I give to others.

○ ○○ 33) I am grateful for my life.

○ ○○ 34) I am grateful for my relationships.

○ ○○ 35) I am grateful for where I am today.

O O O 36) I expect efficiency in everything I do.

O O O 37) I picture myself as a confident person.

O O O 38) I am a confident person.

O O O 39) I am a responsible person.

O O O 40) I am an assertive person.

O O O 41) I have a good balance of exercise and diet.

O O O 42) I have a good balance of work and recreation.

O O O 43) I develop my motivation from within.

O O O 44) I use imaginary rehearsal to view an outcome.

O O O 45) I associate with positive people.

O O O 46) I am a "take-action" type of person.

O O O 47) I have put myself in "someone else's shoes."

O O O 48) I have spoken to a group of more than ten people.

O O O 49) I enjoy speaking and engaging an audience.

O O O 50) I am a member of a toastmasters club.

☛ STEP TWO. DECIDE WHAT IT IS YOU WANT.

What do you want to do with your life? Most people go through life without giving this much thought. To them, a job is employment to make money so that they can live. They eventually become victims of their own circumstances,which they have created due to lack of forethought. Some people know from an early age so this step is clear in their minds. Organize your wants, desires, and dreams on paper. This may be hard, but with a little effort and organization you'll be able to clarify where you want to go or what you want to achieve. Whether you are in a career now and want to change, or unsure of which direction you would like to pursue, the following questions will help you organize your thoughts.

A great way to do this thought organization is to list the following questions, leaving a space between each for your answers. Write down as many answers as you can.

What would you like to accomplish this year?

What are the things you enjoy doing most?

What have you succeeded at in the past?

What are you good at?

What do your friends think you are good at?(Usually when you are good at something, you enjoy it.)

Where would you like to be in five years?

Where would you like to be in twenty years?

What careers interest you?

What kinds of relationships would you like to have?

Where have you traveled?

What did you enjoy during your school years?

Make your answers detailed. Instead of just school, was it math or science that you enjoyed? Instead of sports, was it basketball or badminton?

When you finish this exercise, you should have a lot of answers. Now prioritize each answer by giving it a value from 1 to 5. Next, spend the most time with the highest priorities. Think about these answers, visualize and imagine what taking a certain direction would be like.Discuss these topics with friends, colleagues, relatives, and even with people that are in that occupation. Gradually eliminate your topics and you will begin to arrive at one that has remained in your mind because of your interest and forethought.

☛ STEP THREE. PICK A ROLE MODEL

Now that you have arrived at something you want to succeed at, the fastest, most efficient way to proceed is to find people who have already been there, done that. You will want to emulate what they have done to reach that goal. Do not try to reinvent the wheel at this point, but capitalize on avoiding mistakes that others have made in the past. Model yourself after these individuals—how they do what they do, why they do what they do. There is a reason why they do what they do. It is either because they have learned from someone else as you are doing, or they have reached where they are by trial and error. The shortest, most efficient route is having a mentor. You can benefit from your mentor's expertise. The next best route is copying someone you feel is a success at what you want to achieve. You might want to talk to one of these people. It's amazing how much a successful person will tell you if you are willing to listen.

☞ STEP FOUR. DEVELOP A PLAN

You have defined yourself and you know what skills you have to add to your life. You have decided what it is that you want. You have selected one or more people to study that you feel are successful in this area. It is now time to put pen to paper and develop your plan. Read chapter 2 on setting goals again. You are going to back up from your intended achievement to now. Begin with a simple one-page flowchart with a small box at the top indicating where you are now. Two good source examples for this step are listed below. Put a box at the bottom of the page that shows where you want to be. You have just built the skeleton of your plan. Now begin to connect the boxes with a series of lines and boxes. These boxes may contain your subgoals. You can have boxes coming off of these boxes, indicating goals you need to achieve to reach the next level. You can take this one-page outline and expand it to a full picture board or use a four-by-six-foot white board. See chapter 31. We think in pictures, so put your future-dominant thoughts in pictures. You are building your plan and adding to it all the routes that will lead you to success.

Website Flowchart Examples

www.rff.com/flowchart-examples

www.smartdraw.com/examples

☞ STEP FIVE. TAKE ACTION

Imagination is only fantasy unless it is followed by action. You have now laid out your plan of action from big goals back down to immediate smaller ones. See chapter 2. Now it is time to put your self-discipline to work by taking immediate action on your goals. You will want to discipline yourself each day to take action on your plan until it becomes a habit. The reason some people don't succeed usually shows itself at this point in their overall plan. They do not have the self-discipline to adhere to the schedule they have set. The years of an instant-gratification environment have instilled an "I want it now" mindset; this makes it more difficult to stay on course. When your desire and passion come from within, then so will on the motivation you need to complete your action plans.

INDEX

RECOMMENDED READING

Allen, James. *As a Man Thinketh.* New York: Penguin Group,2008.

Atkinson, William W. *Thought Vibration, or the Law of Attraction in the Thought World.* New York: Kessinger Publishing, 1998.

Bailey, Simon T. *Release Your Brilliance.* New York: HarperCollins, 2008.

Barker, Raymond C. *Power of Decision.*3rd ed. Los Angeles: DeVorss& Co., 1997.

Betts, George H. *The Distribution and Functions of Mental Imagery.* New York: AMS Press, 1972.

Blakeslie, Thomas R. *The Right Brain.* New York: Berkley Books, 1986.

Borg, James. *Persuasion.*London: Prentice Hall, 2007.

Bristol, Claude. *The Magic of Believing.* New York: Pocket Books, 1994.

Chilton, David. *The Wealthy Barber.* Roseville, CA: Prima Publishing, 1998.

Chopra, Deepak. *The Spontaneous Fulfillment of Desire.* New York: Harmony, 2003.

Covey, Stephen R. *The 7 Habits of Highly Effective People.* New York: Free Press, 2004.

————.*First Things First.* New York: Free Press, 2003.

Dyer, Dr. Wayne W. *Inspiration.*Carlsbad, CA: Hay House, 2006.

Gitomer, Jeffrey. *Little Black Book of Connections.* Austin: Bard Press, 2006.

————. *Little Red Book of Selling.*Austin: Bard Press, 2005.

Hicks, Esther and Jerry. *The Amazing Power of Deliberate Thinking.* Carlsbad, CA: Hay House, 2006.

Hill, Napoleon. *Think and Grow Rich.* New York: Fawcett Books, 1990.

Holmes, Ernest. *Science of Mind.* New York: J.P. Tarcher, 1998.

Lorayne, Harry. *Secrets of Mind Power.* New York: Frederick Fell, 1961.

Maltz, Maxwell. *The New Psycho-Cybernetics.* New York: Prentice Hall, 2001.

Mesmer, Robert. *A Super Powerful Memory Can Be Yours.* Canada: Mirage Publishing, 2008.

————. *The Power of Visualization.* Canada: Mirage Publishing, 2007.

Murphy, Dr. Joseph. *The Power of Your Subconscious Mind.* New York: Bantam, 2001.

Peale, Norman Vincent. *The Power of Positive Thinking.* New York: Ballantine, 1952.

Proctor, Bob. *You Were Born Rich.* Toronto, Proctor, 1999.

Robbins, Anthony. *Awaken the Giant Within.* New York: Summit, 1991.

Schwartz, David. *The Magic of Thinking Big.* New York: Fireside Publishing, 1987.

Sharma, Robin. *The Greatness Guide, Book 2.* Toronto: HarperCollins, 2007.

Stanley, Thomas. *The Millionaire Mind.* Kansas City: Andrews McMeel, 2001.

Staples, Dr. Walter D. *Think like a Winner.*Los Angeles: Wilshire, 1993.

Tracy, Brian. *Change Your Thinking, Change Yourself.* Hoboken, NJ: John Wiley, 2003.

———. *Life Goals!*Wiiliston, VT:Berrett-Koehler, 2003.

———. *Create Your Own Future.* Hoboken, NJ: John Wiley, 2002.

Vitale, Dr. Joe. *The Attractor Factor.* Hoboken, NJ: John Wiley, 2005.

Vorderman, Carol. *Super Brain.* Toronto: Penguin, 2007.

Wattles, Wallace. *The Science of Getting Rich.*Largo, FL: Top of the Mountain Publishing, 1910.

ABOUT THE AUTHOR

Robert Mesmer is an author, speaker, teacher, and entertainer. He taught high school for thirty-two years with major subjects of law, psychology, journalism, and art. During that period, he developed a successful import/export business, which he eventually sold to his two partners. Never a person to stand still, Robert has made a lifelong study of hypnosis and its application to life. He toured the country on several occasions with his Hypnotic Seminars on smoking, weight loss, and stress.

Robert has produced over twenty-four CDs on hypnosis and authored five books on different self help topics. After leaving the teaching in the schools, he toured the New Zealand Theatre circuit with his Hypnotic Show. He traveled the world for five years as a headline act on Princess Cruises. Robert is now focusing on his in-demand speaking engagements in the corporate and college environment. His years on stage as a performer and his continuing exhaustive search for self-help strategies make for a very informative and entertaining presentation. Robert believes that everyone has untapped abilities and talents. He will show you how to find yours and how to use them.

Robert Mesmer books are available at quantity discounts for orders of ten or more copies.

THE

POWER

OF

VISUALIZATION

You Can

Harness Images to

Persuade Others

& Create Success

In Your Life

Robert Mesmer

Available in audio book and e-book formats.

To find out about discounts for orders of 10 or more copies for individuals, corporations, institutions and organizations please contact us through our Website at www.robertmesmer.com.

To receive Robert's FREE monthly e-newsletter, chock-full of information to improve your life and take you to the next level, go to www.robertmesmer.com

A

SUPER

POWERFUL

MEMORY

Can Be Yours

The Secret to Memory

An Improved Memory in Minutes

Robert Mesmer

Available in audio book and ebook formats.

To find out about discounts for orders of 10 or more copies for individuals, corporations, institutions, and organizations please contact us through our Website at www.robertmesmer.com.

To receive Robert's FREE monthly e-newsletter, chock-full of information to improve your life and take you to the next level, go to www.robertmesmer.com

INVEST IN YOURSELF

ROBERT MESMER

Speaker–Author–Educator–Performer

To book Robert as a speaker at your event, contact

Robert Mesmer International LLC ™

at

www.robertmesmer.com

Printed in the United States
by Baker & Taylor Publisher Services